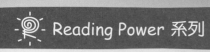

Reading Power 系列

108 課綱、全民英檢中級／中高級、
TOEIC 新多益英語測驗適用
可搭配 108 課綱選修課程

Effective English:
Skills for Practical Reading Comprehension

活用英文：

實用英文閱讀訓練

附解析本

王信雲、李秋芸 編著　Ian Fletcher 審定

編著者
王信雲
學歷：國立陽明交通大學英語教學研究所碩士
經歷：桃園市立壽山高級中學英語科教師

李秋芸
學歷：國立陽明交通大學英語教學研究所碩士
經歷：國立新竹高級中學英語科教師

審定者
Ian Fletcher
學歷：英國牛津大學文學碩士
經歷：英語教師、自由作家

三民書局

序

知識，就是希望；閱讀，就是力量。

在這個資訊爆炸的時代，應該如何選擇真正有用的資訊來吸收？

在考場如戰場的競爭壓力之下，應該如何儲備實力，漂亮地面對挑戰？

身為地球村的一分子，應該如何增進英語實力，與世界接軌？

學習英文的目的，就是要讓自己在這個資訊爆炸的時代之中，突破語言的藩籬，站在吸收新知的制高點之上，以閱讀獲得力量，以知識創造希望！

針對在英文閱讀中可能面對的挑戰，我們費心規劃 Reading Power 系列叢書，希望在學習英語的路上助你一臂之力，讓你輕鬆閱讀、快樂學習。

誠摯希望在學習英語的路上，這套 Reading Power 系列叢書將伴隨你找到閱讀的力量，發揮知識的光芒！

給讀者的話

　　臺灣教育正逐漸跨越出過去課程綱要所強調的「課程知識」，而是強調所謂的「核心素養」。在國教院所提出的「十二年國民基本教育領域課程綱要」中，「核心素養」指的是「一個人為適應現在生活及未來挑戰，所應具備的知識、能力與態度」，其概念強調學習者不以「學科知識」為唯一的學習範疇，而是能培養出其與情境結合並在生活中實踐力行的特質，並成功地回應個人或社會的生活需求。

　　因此，以素養為導向的命題方式，將逐漸擺脫過去著墨於知識和理解層次的紙筆考試，而強調接近真實世界的情境與問題。簡言之，素養命題幫助學習者拋棄機械式地背誦學習，盼其獲得可應用於真實情境中的問題解決能力。

　　本書以上述素養命題原則為本，將學習者的生活經驗概略區分為「旅遊交通」、「生活」、「飲食」和「大眾傳播」四大面向。題幹不見得冗長，但放入大量貼近真實生活的符號、多元表徵、媒體識讀與運用的系統性題目。盼本書能使學習者真實運用「直接提取」（理解文中的基本詞彙及關鍵訊息、解讀文中語句的意義與關係、掌握文本大意）、「推論分析」（解讀文中的人事物關係、依據文本訊息之關聯度來猜測）、「詮釋整合」（判斷因果關係、分析與歸納全文大意）及「比較評估」（能類推原則、預測結果、找出問題解決的方法）四大能力，使英語文不只侷限於知識性記憶和背誦，而成為跨領域、跨學科的問題解決工具。

王信雲、李秋芸

CONTENTS

01 旅遊交通
Travel & Transportation

Read the business card and answer the questions.

**Sanmin City
Transportation Department**

Till Teuber

Chief of Traffic Control and Engineering Division
Maintaining high standards in traffic control and
engineering for the city transportation

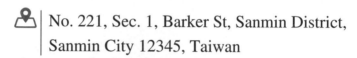 No. 221, Sec. 1, Barker St, Sanmin District,
Sanmin City 12345, Taiwan

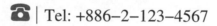 Tel: +886–2–123–4567

_____ 1. **Where does Mr. Teuber work?**

(A) At a bus station.

(B) At a police bureau.

(C) At a government office.

(D) At an engineering company.

_____ 2. **Which of the following might be Mr. Teuber's duties at work?**

(A) Selling vehicles.

(B) Repairing cars.

(C) Executing traffic policies.

(D) Beautifying the city with seasonal decorations.

_____ 3. **What is NOT the purpose of this card?**

(A) To introduce Mr. Teuber.

(B) To indicate Mr. Teuber's career specialty.

(C) To remind people of Mr. Teuber's e-mail address.

(D) To inform people of Mr. Teuber's office address.

_____ 4. Information about the motor vehicle population and density in Sanmin City is presented in the following table. What information **CANNOT** be found in this table?

	Year	Motor Vehicle Population			Motor Vehicle Density (vehicles/km^2)		
		Totality	Cars	Scooters	Totality	Cars	Scooters
Sanmin City	2011	3,284,713	924,938	2,359,775	1,600.30	450.63	1,149.67
	2012	3,309,078	940,167	2,368,911	1,612.17	458.04	1,154.12
	2013	3,233,275	964,136	2,269,139	1,575.24	469.72	1,105.51
	2014	3,178,499	987,361	2,191,138	1,548.55	481.04	1,067.51
	2015	3,183,551	1,005,501	2,178,050	1,551.01	489.87	1,061.13
	2016	3,193,363	1,013,041	2,180,322	1,555.79	493.55	1,062.24
	2017	3,207,823	1,017,211	2,190,612	1,562.83	495.58	1,067.25

(A) The changes of user density over time.

(B) The ratios of cars to scooters.

(C) The increase in the car population.

(D) The decrease in the scooter density.

5. Based on the table above, give a probable explanation for higher density of cars but lower density of overall motor vehicles.

_____

_____

Read the sign and answer the questions.

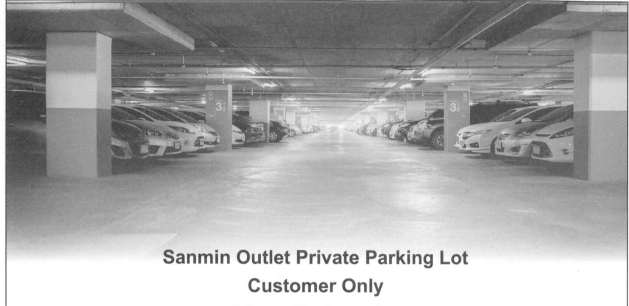

Sanmin Outlet Private Parking Lot
Customer Only
2 Hours Maximum Stay

This parking lot is patrolled. Unauthorized vehicles will be towed away. Failure to comply with the following regulations may result in the issue of an NT$800 parking charge notice.

🕐 Parking limited to 2 hours (No return within 2 hours)

🚗 Parking only within marked bays

👪 Parent & child parking only within marked bays (The driver must be accompanied by a child.)

♿ Disabled bays are for disabled badge holders only (Valid badge must be displayed. No concessions are made for disable badge holders.)

_____ 1. Where can people see the sign?

(A) In a parking area near the city hall.

(B) At the parking lot of a shopping mall.

(C) In a residents' parking zone.

(D) At the parking space in a middle school.

_____ 2. Which of the following situations would **NOT** cause a parking penalty charge?

(A) Re-entry within 1 hour.

(B) Use parent and child parking space without being accompanied by a child.

(C) Park within designated areas.

(D) Park in disabled bays without disabled badges on the car.

_____ 3. One woman enters the parking lot with two children. Where should she park her car?

(A) In a VIP parking zone.

(B) In a disabled parking area.

(C) In an unpatrolled parking space.

(D) In a marked parking spot.

4. According to the situation below, why did the lady face a penalty fine?

One store was accused of fining shoppers NT$800 when they were spotted using parent-and-children spaces without a child under the age of 12 by their side. One woman who was handed a ticket said, "I found the parking attendant and his manager to question the decision. They were incredibly rude and told me I didn't count as a parent yet."

The store then explained that only drivers with their children by their side are allowed to park in the parent-and-child spaces, and that's why the lady received a ticket.

_____

_____

Read the information and answer the questions.

PARKING RATES

Monday to Friday

First 3 hours or part thereof ··· $150

Subsequent hour or part thereof ··· $50/h

Maximum per entry per day ··· $600

Saturday, Sunday, Public Holiday and Eve of Public Holiday

First 2 hours or part thereof ··· $300

Subsequent HALF an hour ··· $50

Lost Ticket ··· $1,000

Notice:

1. Operating hours: 6:00 a.m.–12:00 midnight.
2. Users leaving their cars in the parking lot until it reopens will be charged a flat fee of $1,500 per night.
3. The above parking rates are inclusive of 6% GST (Goods-and-Service Tax).

_____ 1. **For at least how many hours of parking will a driver get before paying the maximum parking fee during weekdays?**

  (A) 15 hours.

  (B) 12 hours.

  (C) 9 hours.

  (D) 6 hours.

_____ 2. **On December 24th, the Wangs went for Christmas shopping and parked their car for 4 hours. When they were about to leave, they found the parking ticket had gone. How much should they pay?**

(A) $400.

(B) $1,000.

(C) $1,400.

(D) $1,500.

_____ 3. **On 1:00 a.m. January 1st, the security guard found an overnight parking car. Through the monitor, he noticed that this car had entered the parking lot at 6:00 p.m. the day before. At 6:00 am, a group of young people claimed that they had parked the car overnight for the countdown party nearby. How much should they pay in total?**

(A) $500.

(B) $850.

(C) $1,700.

(D) $2,200.

4. **What does "First 3 hours or part thereof" mean? Explain in your own words.**

_____

_____

_____

Read the notice and answer the questions.

Road Resurfacing Notice

The City Hall will be resurfacing the roadway on King's Road from the Route 236 to Park Avenue East. This project is part of the Council Approved 2018 Road Resurfacing Program. Your cooperation and patience during the construction period is appreciated.

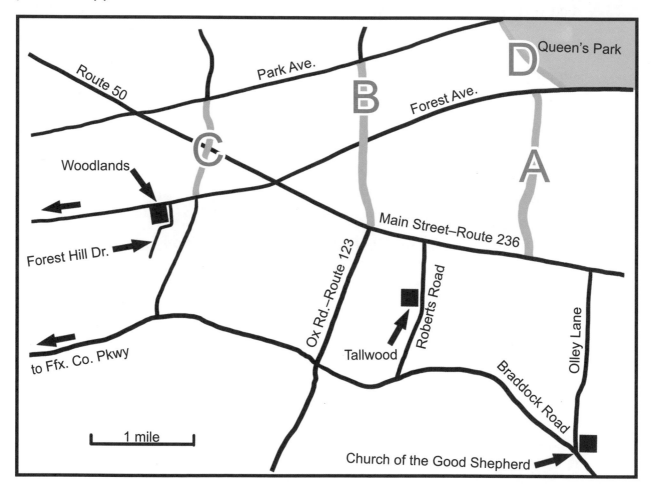

Details:

The work is as follows:

- Repairing and resurfacing road surface.

- Sidewalk and curb repairs, pavement markings, driveway restoration, and lawn replacement.

- The work also includes improving pedestrian crossings at the intersections along this section.

Notice:

Temporary lane closures and parking restrictions **adjacent to** construction zones will be in effect. Access to nearby areas might not be available; passing vehicles are subject to traffic regulations during the construction.

_____ 1. Which of the following roads will be under construction?

(A) Road A.

(B) Road B.

(C) Road C.

(D) Road D.

_____ 2. Which of the following work is **NOT** included in this project?

(A) Curb Removal.

(B) Crosswalk striping.

(C) Grassland replacement.

(D) Road Surface Marking.

_____ 3. Javier: I can't believe I forget the resurfacing today!

Martina: That's why you are so late.

Javier: Yeah, I thought I could turn left onto King's Road and then turn right at the intersection of King's Road and Forest Avenue, but I was wrong.

Martina: So, how did you come here?

Javier: I had to go another 2 miles east and then go a long way north to Queen's Park where I could finally turn onto Forest Avenue.

Martina: Oh! Poor you.

According to the conversation and the notice above, which of the following is the right compass direction on this map?

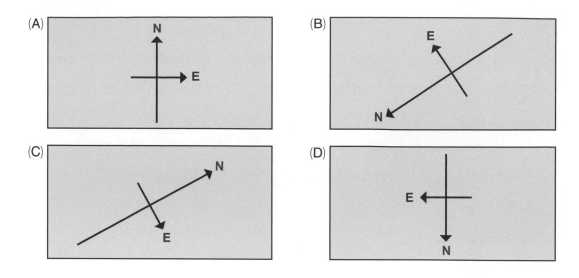

_____ 4. Which of the following meanings is closest to the phrase "adjacent to" in the last part of the notice?

(A) Near.

(B) Remote.

(C) Beyond.

(D) Opposite to.

5. It is reported that a public school will be built in the region enclosed by King's Road, Forest Ave., and Main Street. Crosshatch the designated area on the following map.

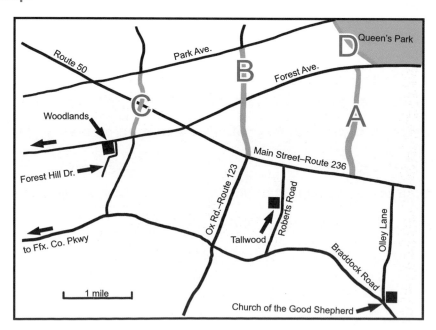

NOTES

Read the announcement and answer the questions.

"During takeoff, landing, and adverse weather conditions like turbulence, the seat belt sign will illuminate. To ensure your safety, you must fasten your seat belt by inserting the metal fitting into the buckle, and pulling on the loose end of the strap to tighten it. To release your seat belt, lift the upper portion of the buckle.

Once a decision has been made to evacuate, floor-level lighting will guide you toward the nearest exit, which is normally the one behind you. Move the handle in the direction of the arrow to open the door, which may also be detached and used as a life raft as it is equipped with an inflatable slide inside.

During severe hazards in flight, you may pull the oxygen mask toward you, and place it firmly over your nose and mouth to breathe oxygen normally. Secure your mask first before you assist another person.

When instructed to use a life vest located in a pouch under your seat or between the armrests, open the plastic pouch and remove the vest. To put on the vest, you must slip it over your head, pass the straps around your waist, and adjust it at the front. Only when leaving the aircraft do you need to inflate the vest by pulling firmly on the red cord. If your vest fails to inflate, blow into the mouthpieces.

Finally, we remind you that this is a non-smoking cabin. We wish you all an enjoyable trip."

_____ 1. In what kind of vehicles may passengers hear this announcement?

(A) Trains.　　　　　　　　　　　(B) Airplanes.

(C) Tour buses.　　　　　　　　　(D) Cruise ships.

_____ 2. What is the purpose of this announcement?

(A) To make a takeoff notice.

(B) To remind platform alteration.

(C) To explain safety demonstration.

(D) To give delayed service information.

_____ 3. Which of the following information is **NOT** mentioned in this announcement?

(A) Evacuation procedure.

(B) Life vest usage directions.

(C) Seat belt usage instructions.

(D) Passenger insurance application.

_____ 4. **Where would the sentence "In the event of decompression, an oxygen mask will automatically appear in front of you." best fit?**

Oxygen and the air pressure are always being monitored. ① To start the flow of oxygen, pull the mask toward you. Place it firmly over your nose and mouth, secure the elastic band behind your head, and breathe normally. ② Although the bag does not inflate, oxygen is flowing to the mask. ③ If you are travelling with a child or someone who requires assistance, secure your mask first, and then assist another person. ④ Keep your mask on until a uniformed crew member advises you to remove it.

(A) ①

(B) ②

(C) ③

(D) ④

Read the diagrams and answer the questions.

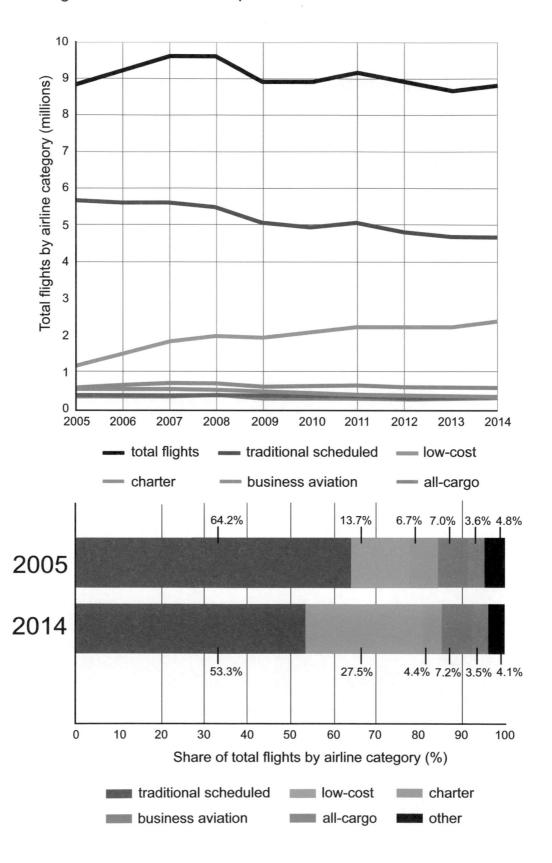

_____ 1. What is the purpose of the diagrams above?

    (A) To show the national airport noise contour.

    (B) To present the steady growth in total flights.

    (C) To illustrate the rise of the average aircraft age.

    (D) To indicate the growth and decline in a series of flights.

_____ 2. Based on the diagrams above, which of the following statements is true?

    (A) There was a growth in cargo flights in 2012 and 2013.

    (B) The charter flights eventually outnumber all the other flights.

    (C) The total number of all aircrafts remained constant over ten years.

    (D) The share of low-cost flights had nearly doubled from 2005 to 2014.

3. In which year did the number of the total flights reach the lowest point?

_____

4. Which kind of flight experienced a slight increase in number in 2012?

_____

Read the timetable and answer the questions.

  086 8626734

June, July & August

Monday to Friday
Depart Whiddy
8:30, 11:00, 13:45, 15:45, 17:45
Depart Bantry
9:30, 11:30, 14:00, 16:00, 18:00
Saturday
Depart Whiddy
9:00, 10:45, 13:45, 15:45, 17:45
Depart Bantry
9:30, 11:00, 13:00, 14:00, 16:00, 18:00
Sunday
Depart Whiddy
11:15, 13:15, 14:15, 16:15, 17:45
Depart Bantry
11:00, 13:00, 14:00, 15:00, 16:00, 18:00

September to May

Monday, Wednesday & Friday
Depart Whiddy
8:30, 11:00, 13:45, 15:45, 17:45
Depart Bantry
9:30, 11:30, 14:00, 16:00, 18:00
Tuesday & Thursday
Depart Whiddy
8:30, 13:45, 15:45, 17:45
Depart Bantry
9:30, 14:00, 16:00, 18:00
Saturday
Depart Whiddy
9:00, 10:45, 13:45, 17:45
Depart Bantry
9:30, 11:00, 14:00, 18:00
Sunday
Depart Whiddy
11:15, 14:15, 17:45
Depart Bantry
11:00, 14:00, 18:00

Harbor Cruises
Trip around Bantry Harbor weekdays at 12:30
Saturday 11:30 and 16:30
Sunday 12:00
Evening cruise 19:00 by arrangement

Extra Trips by arrangement
New Year Holiday Trips

Please get on board 5 mins before departure.

_____ 1. Based on the timetable above, what type of transportation is the means of conveyance of passengers?

(A) Ferries.

(B) Trains.

(C) Tour buses.

(D) Airplanes.

2. It's July, and this Saturday, Mason is going to a party near the harbor. He intends to leave the party at 17:50 and go to the harbor to catch transportation. Which harbor might he be heading to?

_____

3. How many trips are at least provided per day during the off seasons (September to May)?

_____

_____ 4. Sharmila is inviting her friends to an evening harbor cruise this Sunday. What time should she write on the invitation to make sure her guests get on board on time?

(A) 8:55.

(B) 11:55.

(C) 15:55.

(D) 18:55.

Read the mail and answer the questions.

New message _ ⌞⌝ ✕

To

Subject

Dear Ms. Wang,

Further to our latest correspondence, we have investigated the concerns which you raised with regards to your booking for the cruise vacation to the Maldives. Based on our findings, there was a system **glitch** where the wrong exchange rate was used in the calculation which resulted in you making a payment much less than the original fare offered.

To that end, as a gesture of goodwill we will honor the booking which you made. Please be informed that we have sent the electronic tickets and the itinerary receipt to you.

Regards,
Michael
Customer Care Division

☰ | A ⌀ 🖾 ⚬ ☺ | ★ 🗑   Send

---

1. **What is the purpose of this mail?**

_____

_____

_____

_____ 2. **In which company might Michael work?**

    (A) Bikefarm.

    (B) Continental Railways.

    (C) Mega Maldives Airlines.

    (D) Royal Ocean Carnival.

_____ 3. **Which piece of information is NOT mentioned in this mail?**

(A) The wrong fare will be accepted by the company.

(B) The accepted price is lower than the original one.

(C) The incorrect destination is caused by some system mistakes.

(D) There was an unexpected technical problem that caused an incorrect payment to be made.

_____ 4. **Based on this mail, how will Ms. Wang get her tickets?**

(A) She will get the tickets in the local agency.

(B) Her tickets will be sent as registered mail.

(C) Her tickets will be enclosed in the notification letter.

(D) She will get her tickets as attached files in an e-mail.

_____ 5. **What does the word "glitch" mean?**

(A) A minor problem.

(B) A reduction in the price.

(C) An act to increase sales.

(D) An update to include the latest information.

Read the letter and answer the questions.

New message   _ ⌐ ×

To:

Subject:

Dear Ms. Wang,

Thank you for choosing to stay with us at the Premier Hotel. We are pleased to confirm your reservation as follows:

Guest Name:	Ms. Jill Wang	**Confirmation Number:**	123456
Arrival Date:	2/14/2025	**Departure Date:**	2/16/2025
Number of Guests:	2	**Accommodations:**	**Deluxe King Suite**
		Rate per Night:	**$3,500**
Check-in Time:	15:00	**Check-out Time:**	12:00

Notice: Additional 15% rates are subjected to applicable local taxes.

If you require an early check-in, please make your request as soon as possible. We won't charge fees if you request in advance.

If you find it necessary to cancel the reservation, the Premier Hotel requires notification by 16:00 the day before your arrival to avoid a charge for one night's room rate.

If you want us to do anything to make your visit extra special, call us at 02–12345678. Or by clicking Contact Concierge here, you will be taken to our pre-arrival checklist from where we will assist you with advance reservation for airport transfers, dining, golf tee-times, and spa treatments.

We look forward to the pleasure of having you as our guest at the Premier Hotel.

Sincerely,
David Chen

_____ 1. **What is the purpose of this letter?**

(A) To confirm the reservation.

(B) To remind the guest to pay.

(C) To promote the tour package.

(D) To explain the booking process.

_____ 2. **Which division of the hotel does Mr. Chen possibly work for?**

(A) Stewarding.

(B) Housekeeping.

(C) Human Resources.

(D) Reservation and Front Office.

_____ 3. **Based on the information provided, what service may the Premier Hotel NOT offer?**

(A) Spa and fitness.

(B) Transportation.

(C) Food and beverage.

(D) Folklore events.

4. **How much shall Ms. Wang pay for her two-night stay at the Premier Hotel?**

_____

_____ 5. **According to this letter, which piece of information is NOT correct?**

(A) Ms. Wang may enjoy her free early check-in.

(B) Ms. Wang will pay more than $7,000 for her two-night stay.

(C) Ms. Wang may cancel her reservation on the day they arrive.

(D) Ms. Wang may contact the Premier Hotel via online checklists.

Read the information and answer the questions.

SanMin

Plan **A** NT$ **200**
2 days
2 days (48 hours) of unlimited data service once registered in Taiwan

Plan **B** NT$ **350**
5 days + free voice call NT$50
5 days (120 hours) of unlimited data service once registered in Taiwan

Plan **C** NT$ **400**
5 days + free voice call NT$150
5 days (120 hours) of unlimited data service once registered in Taiwan

Plan **D** NT$ **450**
7 days + free voice call NT$200
7 days (168 hours) of unlimited data service once registered in Taiwan

Plan **E** NT$ **450**
8 days + free voice call NT$100
8 days (192 hours) of unlimited data service once registered in Taiwan

Plan **F** NT$ **500**
10 days + free voice call NT$100
10 days (240 hours) of unlimited data service once registered in Taiwan

Plan **G** NT$ **800**
15 days + free voice call NT$250
15 days (360 hours) of unlimited data service once registered in Taiwan

Plan **H** NT$ **1000**
30 days + free voice call NT$430
30 days (720 hours) of unlimited data service once registered in Taiwan

SanMin

_____ 1. Which of the following products best fits the above characteristics?

(A) Cellphone plans.

(B) Karaoke machines.

(C) Streaming music apps.

(D) Cable TV bundles and packages.

_____ 2. Which of the following plans fits the package description?

Only NT$50 per day! Unlimited 4G high speed Internet brings you an unlimited overseas experience. For just NT$500 for 10 days, you can use the Internet as much as you want. You can get additional free NT$100 voice calls. Planning a trip abroad? Choose the Sanmin Mobile right now!

(A) Plan B.

(B) Plan F.

(C) Plan G.

(D) Plan H.

3. Jade will visit her relatives in Taiwan next month. She will stay there for 15 days and need to use the Internet for the whole trip. She estimates that she will spend about NT$250 on voice calls. What is the most economical combination plan?

02 生活
Living & Lifestyle

Dear Mr. Leading

Recently, I've been bombarded with this annoying alert.

> 💣 **SETTINGS**   **now**
> **Backup Failed**
> You do not have enough space in Cloud to back up this phone.

I spent NT$21,000 buying this "outstanding" phone, and you gave me just 5GB of free Cloud storage. I bought this so-called "leading" smartphone during your sale season, and all of your advertising campaigns kept persuading consumers that "our product is outstanding not only for its huge amount of storage but also for its automatic backup—consumers won't lose much at all if they accidentally lose their phones, for their photos, videos, contacts, and more will be safely stored in Cloud." However, I've only been using your product for two weeks, and there are already problems. My available Cloud space is already running low after only one week of taking photos and videos. I'm highly dissatisfied with your product and service. **Tell me, how can I survive with only 5GB of storage space?**

Yours truly,

Dianna Johns

Ms. Johns,

Thank you for your message. We are sorry for bothering you with our **notifications**. We provide every customer with five gigabytes of free Cloud storage space, but if you do need more, we also offer other options. We offer customers alternative plans: NT$60 a month for 100GB, NT$90 for 300GB, and NT$150 for 1TB. A new Cloud storage family sharing plan will also be available if you decide on the latter two plans.

Understandably, you may have decided not to spend more on online storage since you've spent NT$21,000 on our product. Therefore, we suggest you regularly download all the files from your Cloud to any of your storage devices and then delete all of them. By doing so, you can still ensure a safe and accessible space of 5GB online storage where you can access what you have stored by logging in.

Finally, many thanks for your understanding, and have a nice day.

Yours sincerely,

Leading Phone

_____ 1. **Why did Dianna Johns write this message?**

(A) She complained about the functions of her new smartphone.

(B) She was angry at the poor customer service.

(C) She wished to have larger free online backup space.

(D) She was asking to return her new smartphone.

_____ 2. **Which of the following about the response of Leading Phone to Dianna Johns is true?**

(A) The company offered her alternative plans.

(B) The company promised to lengthen the warranty.

(C) The company blamed the fault on her ignorance.

(D) The company admitted its inadequate service.

3 **What is closest in meaning to the underlined word "notifications"?**

(A) Campaigns.   (B) Files.

(C) Alternatives.   (D) Alerts.

_____ 4. **What did Dianna Johns mean by saying, "Tell me, how can I survive with only 5GB of storage space?"**

(A) She tried to bargain with the company for extra space.

(B) She was planning to buy a new smartphone from another brand.

(C) She was looking for someone who survived with 5GB of Cloud space.

(D) She had convinced herself to use only 5GB of Cloud space.

5. **What is the least fee Diana Johns would pay if she wanted to share her Cloud storage space with her family?**

02

Bring Greenery to Work

Keep pot plants on your desk or around it, which can help make your office green and eco-friendly, reduce indoor toxic air, and lower your stress level.

Don't Waste Food

Think before you act. One-third of the world's food gets wasted. Before throwing anything away, think about those hungry people who live in places where there isn't enough food or resources.

Say No to Printing

Avoid printing in color or try to print double-sided. Use e-mail and Cloud to share documents.

Conserve Energy

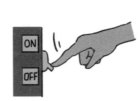

Turn off all electronic appliances and gadgets when not in use. Unplug your mobile chargers while they are not being used. Turn off the lights when leaving rooms.

Recycle

Turn used paper into recycled paper. Used bottles and cartons can be repurposed to make beautiful crafts.

Bike/Carpool to Work

Cycling is healthy and eco-friendly. Carpooling can also save money and reduce carbon dioxide emissions, making it an environmentally friendly option.

Conserve Water

If the toilet is clean, there is no need to flush it before use. Avoid keeping the tap on while not using the water. Use recyclable water to flush.

Avoid Disposable Cups

Think of the huge garbage islands floating in the Pacific Ocean. Stop using disposable containers, and carry your own reusable bottle or a ceramic mug every time you drink water.

Join Green Initiatives

Never say no to any green initiatives by your company—tree planting, riding a bike to work— Every bit counts.

Lend Your Support

Sign up for environmental events. Help out every way you can—through donations or online petitions. Spread the word on social media. Every voice matters.

_____ 1. Where may people mostly likely see this poster?

(A) On the campus.

(B) At a coffee shop.

(C) In an office.

(D) In the library.

_____ 2. Which is the best title for this poster?

(A) Top 10 Eco-friendly Activities for Students

(B) Let's Develop Green Thumbs at Our Desks!

(C) 10 Things Highly Recommended for a Green Revolution

(D) 10 Easy Ways to Go Green at Work

_____ 3. What does the word "carpool" mean in the passage?

(A) To encourage the purchase of used cars.

(B) To share one car with other people.

(C) To reduce air pollution by buying electric cars.

(D) To conserve energy by riding a bike to work.

_____ 4. Which of the following statements is **NOT** mentioned in the poster?

(A) Disposable containers have increased the workload of cleaners.

(B) Using reusable water bottles or mugs is encouraged for drinking.

(C) Every small change will make a difference to the environment.

(D) A paperless environment is one of the goals we attempt to achieve.

5. As a student, what can you do to help bring greenery to your classroom?

_____

_____

03

Symbols on a care label tag provide helpful information about the garment we are going to buy. The care label describes the proper treatment of the garment without damaging the textile. There is information about how it should be washed with what kind of water temperature setting, or about whether it can be bleached, dried, ironed, and so on. Five basic symbols are often used in the care labeling system (Figure 1).

Figure 1

| Washing | Bleaching | Drying | Ironing | Dry Cleaning |

However, most often, what we read is like this (Figure 2).

Figure 2

MADE IN Canada | **XS**

100% COMBED RING SPUN COTTON PRESHRUNK

Some symbols become more complicated. A rectangular-shaped symbol containing a circle inside means "tumble dryer." Referring to the codes on Figure 3 below, the leftmost symbol on Figure 2 means "tumble dry at a normal temperature." A triangle with two bars inside refers to "only bleaching with oxygen allowed." The more bars a symbol has, the more gently the garment should be treated. Figure 3 shows some codes widely used for symbols in Figure 1.

Figure 3

More Dots → More Heat			More Bars → More Gentle		
●	●●	●●●	—	═	✕
COOL/ LOW	WARM/ MEDIUM	HOT/ HIGH	PERMANENT PRESS CYCLE	GENTLE/ DELICATE CYCLE	DO NOT

What's more, there are also some explicit written messages on the label tag. As is shown in Figure 2, "100% combed ring spun cotton **pre-shrunk**" tells the consumers that the garment is made of cotton and that the clothing has been made smaller by washing before being sold.

Therefore, pay careful attention to the care label tags and follow the directions in order to look after your clothes properly.

1. Draw the symbol for "Do Not Tumble Dry."

_____ 2. What is the main purpose of this passage?

(A) To teach readers how to read a care label tag.

(B) To introduce the history of care label tags.

(C) To compare two different kinds of care labeling.

(D) To promote a new care labeling system.

_____ 3. Which of the following is **NOT** mentioned in the passage?

(A) Functions of a care label tag.

(B) Tips for understanding a care label tag.

(C) Reasons for figuring out symbols on a care label.

(D) Requirements of putting a care label tag on clothes.

_____ 4. What does the underlined word "pre-shrunk" mean?

(A) Being made of some clothing that will shrink due to washing.

(B) Not getting further smaller in size as a result of being washed.

(C) Making it easily recognizable by listing instructions clearly.

(D) Keeping something intact to well preserve the garment.

_____ 5. **Which of the following statements complies with the care label below?**

(A) Hand wash only and do not bleach, dry clean, or iron.

(B) Tumble dry at medium temperature on a gentle cycle.

(C) Wash at a maximum of 40 degrees Celsius on a permanent press cycle.

(D) Iron at low temperature and only bleach with oxygen allowed.

NOTES

04

Jimmy entered Sanmin Amusement Park at noon. After having lunch, he went to a show at East Front. It is now 14:20. Jimmy just finished watching "The Bowman Show" and has already had some rest. Look at the following poster and answer the questions.

_____ 1. **What information does this poster give?**

(A) Detailed information about each show.

(B) Prices for the long-running shows.

(C) Places where people can buy the tickets.

(D) Timetable and location for different shows.

_____ 2. **Which of the following statements is true?**

(A) Jimmy can buy tickets for all the shows at the Great Hall Entrance.

(B) Jimmy can watch "Flight of the Eagles" at The Courtyard Shop anytime.

(C) Jimmy will know when hc can watch "History Tours" at the Great Hall Entrance.

(D) A show called "The Castle Dungeon" is released at the Riverside Arena.

_____ 3. According to Jimmy's schedule, which show is definitely available for him to watch next?

(A) The Mighty Trebuchet.

(B) Flight of the Eagles.

(C) The Castle Dungeon.

(D) None of the above.

4. Below is the map of Sanmin Amusement Park. Draw how Jimmy will go from where he is now to the next show he wants to watch. Besides, based on the given information, explain the reason for your answers to Question 3.

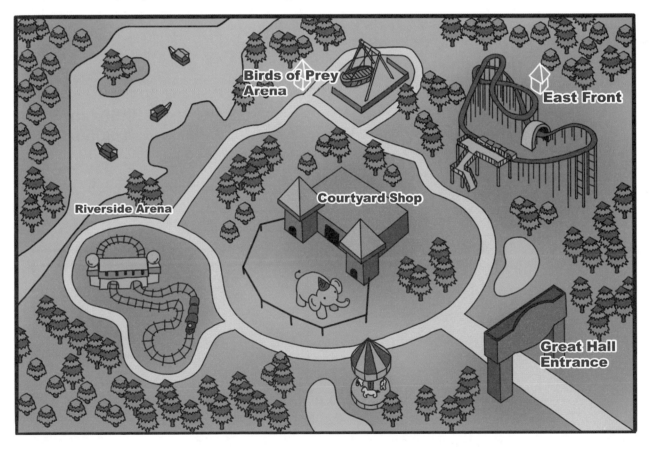

_____

_____

_____

_____

_____

_____

05

You can find us at Tilling Road, Brent Cross NW2 1LW
Tel: 0208 666 1717

We have everything under one roof:
- Full range of toys and games
- Appliances for babies and preschoolers
- Bikes, trikes, and scooters
- Outdoor play, sports, and ride on vehicles
- Technology and video games

Largest toy store in London:
- Free on-site parking
- Car seat check and fitting
- Assembly service available
- Take time to pay facility
- Click and collect @toysfun.co.uk

We are literally at the junction of A41 and A406
From Brent Cross shopping center
✓ Car - 1.1 miles / 7 mins
✓ Bus - 70 or 210 / 20 mins
✓ Underground - Circle Line / 10 mins

OPEN 'TIL LATE

Monday—Friday	9 AM—10 PM
Saturday	9 AM—10 PM
Sunday	11 AM—5 PM

We also have a ToysFun & KidsCome Superstore 12 miles west near Heathrow:
Hayes Bypass, West London. UB2 5LN
Ask one of our advisors for details. Tel: 0208 666 5817

_____ 1. Look at the advertisement for ToysFunKidsCome (TFKC). What is **NOT** mentioned in the ad?

(A) The address of the store.

(B) The business hours of the store.

(C) The vehicles kids can play on outdoors.

(D) The customers' reviews of the store.

2. According to the information given, which family members might be the primary customers frequenting this store?

_____

_____ 3. People always say TFKC are famous for their considerate service. Which of the following is **NOT** offered, according to the ad?

(A) Helping parents take care of their children.

(B) Offering free parking service for customers.

(C) Being open most evenings.

(D) Providing online shopping platform.

_____ 4. Mrs. Peng, who lives nearby in the Brent Cross area, wants to buy trikes for her nephew's birthday. She is told that all the toys are now on sale at the TFKC. Which of the following **CANNOT** be an option for her?

(A) Take bus 70 and 210 to the physical store.

(B) Dial 0208–666–1717 for further information.

(C) Visit the store with her nephew on Sunday night.

(D) Take the Circle Line from the shopping center.

06

Welcome to the Sanmin University Library. You are required to sign the "Terms of User Agreement" before you are allowed to borrow from the library. Before you sign up, please confirm your email address and make sure that you've fully understood all the library's regulations. Here is an important reminder: The library will enforce a recall policy if the item you intend to borrow has also been reserved by others—the borrowing period for the item will be shortened to 14 days. If reservations are made by other users after you have borrowed the item, the item's borrowing period will be changed as follows:

1. For an item that you've borrowed for less than 14 days, the borrowing period will be adjusted to 21 days, and you will be notified of the revised due date via email.

2. For an item that you've borrowed for more than 14 days, please return the item within 7 days after you have received the notification.

If you have any questions and/or suggestions, please contact the circulation desk at 012-01234 (ext. 520) or by email at libservice@smu.edu.tw.

User ID: [ ]

Password: [ ]

Send

_____ 1. Where does this information come from?

(A) A flyer from a bookstore.

(B) A webpage from a library.

(C) A log-in page for an online game.

(D) A complaint letter from a librarian.

_____ 2. Who might have to sign this agreement?

(A) All students and the faculty of Sanmin University.

(B) Sponsors of the construction of Sanmin University.

(C) Whoever wants to borrow from the library for the first time.

(D) Anyone who needs to borrow an item that has been reserved.

_____ 3. Linda eventually succeeds in borrowing the latest volume of her favorite novel series on June 4th. However, she is also informed that someone has reserved the same book on June 4th. When is her due date to return the book?

(A) June 10th.   (B) June 17th.

(C) June 24th.   (D) July 1st.

4. In order to do a report, Willy has borrowed a documentary DVD for half a month. The DVD, however, is reserved by a professor today, June 4th. By what date should Willy return the DVD?

_____

07

The poster below is a billboard announcement outside a cathedral.

September 15, Saturday

A wedding will be held this afternoon, and part of the cathedral will be temporarily closed to visitors from 1:30 PM. The entry price will be adjusted accordingly.

Entry prices (9:30 AM-12:45 PM)

Adult: $9

Concessions: $8

(65+, students with valid ID, children 6–17)

Family: $22

(2 adults & 2 children, or 1 adult & 3 children)

- -

Entry prices (after 12:45 PM)

Adult: $7.50

Concessions: $6.50

(65+, students with valid ID, children 6–17)

Family: $18

(adults & 2 children, or 1 adult & 3 children)

*All under 18 must be accompanied by a responsible adult.

_____ 1. **According to the announcement, who will be the least influenced by this event?**

(A) Tourists who want to see the interior of the cathedral.

(B) Souvenir store clerks inside the cathedral.

(C) Guests who come to attend a cathedral wedding.

(D) Janitors who clean the cathedral weekly.

_____ 2. According to the announcement, which of the following statements is true?

(A) A couple got married in a cathedral.

(B) A wedding banquet will be held at noon.

(C) Some parts of the cathedral will be off-limits from 13:30.

(D) The church is only open to visitors in the morning.

_____ 3. Which of the following is closest in meaning to the underlined word "accordingly"?

(A) As a result.　　　　(B) On purpose.

(C) By accident.　　　　(D) In some ways.

4. 11-year-old Elizabeth is interested in architecture. She invites her parents to visit this cathedral on September 15th. There are five people in her family. Besides her dad and mom, she also has a grandpa over 65 and a toddler brother. They arrive at 1 PM. How much do they need to pay?

_____

08

No ideas about where to go during the summer vacation?

This summer, Sanmin Zoo is launching a nine-week events calendar particularly for kids under 18. On every weekday from July 2 to August 31, parents and children can enjoy varied free activities at the zoo.

Little boys and girls can meet their favorite animal character friends from animations on Mondays. Moviegoers are welcome to see family-fun movies on Tuesdays. Preschoolers are encouraged to bring their favorite animal toy dolls for a check-up by the vets at Sanmin Zoo every Wednesday. Elementary school students can enroll in various courses to paint and learn with friends on Thursdays. Every Friday night, mom and dad can take on a yoga session for relaxation.

Each activity has a special focus on the zoo's mission of inspiring visitors' passion to protect wildlife as well as their habitats and arousing public awareness of climate issues.

_____ 1. Which of the following posters can best describe the above information?

(A)

(B)

(C)

(D)

_____ 2. Why does Sanmin Zoo hold a series of summer activities?

(A) To increase the revenues of the zoo in the summer.

(B) To improve the popularity of the zoo in a short time.

(C) To give voice to wildlife conservation and climate concerns.

(D) To raise funds for the endangered animals at Sanmin Zoo.

Based on the above information, look at the pictures below and answer the following two questions.

_____ 3. Which activity are they taking part in?

(A) Paint Day at the Zoo.

(B) Cartoon Character Meet-and-Greets.

(C) Relaxation with Yoga.

(D) Check-up for Animal Toy Dolls at Wildlife Health Center.

4. Which group of visitors may join this activity?

_____ 5. **Read the information below. Which of the statements about this service is true?**

> Don't worry about the summer heat. Sanmin Zoo welcomes everyone to the zoo with open arms. Every Tuesday, three classic movies are played at Sanmin Zoo Special Events Center (indoors) at 10 a.m.–12 a.m., 2 p.m.–4 p.m., and 6 p.m.–8 p.m., respectively. Food and drinks for purchase prior to the movie will be available. To guarantee a spot, guests are advised to purchase a Fast Pass online for only $1 24 hours prior to the scheduled movie. The Fast Pass confirms admission and allows early access to the Special Events Center 15 minutes prior to the movie. Those who don't have a Fast Pass can wait in line at the zoo, but there is no guarantee of entrance to the event—first come, first served.

(A) Children can greet their favorite characters in this activity.

(B) People can buy a Fast Pass 15 minutes prior to the scheduled movie.

(C) Moviegoers might be very interested in this activity.

(D) It is held at the entrance of the Special Events Center.

NOTES

09

PENALTY NOTICE

City of Sanmin / Infringement Notice

Infringement Act 2010. Infringements Regulations 2016.

Notice to the owner of the vehicle: This is an 'Infringement Notice' in relation to the Road Safety Road Rules 2016.

Infringement Number: 1807000188556

Notice Issued: Sun. 11/19/2023

Offense Time: 10:25 AM

Officer ID: PPA 12

Location of alleged offense: Papaya City Hall, Gettysburg Street

Alleged Offense

Offense No.: R101

Offense: Stopping contrary to a No Stopping Sign

Penalty: NT$600

Due Date: 12/31/2023

Vehicle Details

Reg. Number: ABC 1234

State: Papaya State

Brand: Toyota

1234569876543

The infringement penalty must be paid by the due date.

Failure to pay by the due date may result in further enforcement action and additional costs.

_____ 1. **According to the information above, what can we tell about this form?**

(A) It is a parking permit.

(B) It is a parking receipt.

(C) It is a traffic ticket.

(D) It is a driver's license.

____ 2. What offense was committed?

(A) Drunk driving.

(B) Speeding.

(C) Running a red light.

(D) Illegal parking.

_____ 3. Which of the following statements is **NOT** mentioned in the passage?

(A) A Toyota vehicle violated the rule R101 in Papaya City.

(B) The owner can pay the fine at City Hall on Gettysburg Street.

(C) The violation took place on Gettysburg Street one morning in November.

(D) The police officer whose ID was PPA 12 took charge of this infringement.

4. How much is the fine, and when is the deadline?

10

To Commemorate the Bicentenary of Opening

Dunkeld Bridge

Designed by
Thomas Telford (1757–1834)
First President, Institute of Civil Engineers

Built 1804–09 by
John 4th Duke Of Atholl (1755–1830)
As a Major Element in the Improvement of Highland Roads by
Replacing Two Ferries and Paid by Tolls until Taken Over by the
Roads Authority in 1879

Plaque Unveiled by
John 11th Duke of Atholl
21st May 2009

INSTITUTION OF CIVIL ENGINEERS

PERTH &
KINROSS
COUNCIL

The Tay is the longest river in Scotland, carrying heavier volume than any other river in the British Isles. The ferries crossing the Tay were often in danger in high waters. In 1776, one dreadful accident on the Tay at Dunkeld claimed several lives, which forced the local government to be aware of the long-term threats posed by the Tay. With all the wooden bridges across the Tay at Dunkeld swallowed by floods, the government decided to build a stronger bridge. However, due to a limited budget, the government at the time worked on a private-public partnership scheme: The government paid half, and the local landowner paid the other. The landowner at Dunkeld was the 4th Duke of Atholl. Neither the government officials nor Duke Atholl anticipated the construction costs. As the cost spiraled out of control, becoming far more than the government could pay, the Duke had no choice but to **cough up** the rest of the sum, hence making it necessary to place tolls on the bridge. In return, the government appointed the famous Scottish engineer Thomas Telford to design the bridge, making it both functional—carrying most of the traffic into the Highlands—and elegant—being an arc with a revolutionary design. This was the origin of Dunkeld Bridge.

1. **Why was a private-public partnership scheme carried out on the construction of Dunkeld Bridge?**

_____

_____ 2. **What is the function of the plaque on the bridge?**

(A) It is used to remind people of someone or something important.

(B) It gives tourists directions to nearby tourist attractions.

(C) It tells some funny stories that will go down in history.

(D) It serves as the address of where some celebrities were buried.

_____ 3. **Which of the following about the plaque is true?**

(A) It was made by the offspring of Thomas Telford.

(B) It was set up right after the Dunkeld Bridge was built.

(C) It recorded when the bridge toll stopped being charged.

(D) It was designed by Thomas Telford in 1766.

_____ 4. Which of the following reasons could **NOT** explain why the government was keen to build a bridge over the Tay at Dunkeld?

(A) Ferries on the Tay were often in danger in high waters.

(B) An increase in traffic to the Highlands had been urgent.

(C) The volume of traffic on the Tay was heavy all the time.

(D) Some accidents and natural disasters had taken many people's lives.

_____ 5. Which of the following phrases is closest in meaning to the underlined phrase "cough up"?

(A) Take responsibility.   (B) Spend money.

(C) Give up.   (D) Stop by.

03

飲食
Food & Drink

01

Coffee drinks are made with brewing hot water and ground coffee beans. The following menu shows the differences among 9 coffee drinks and how they are made. Read the menu and answer the questions.

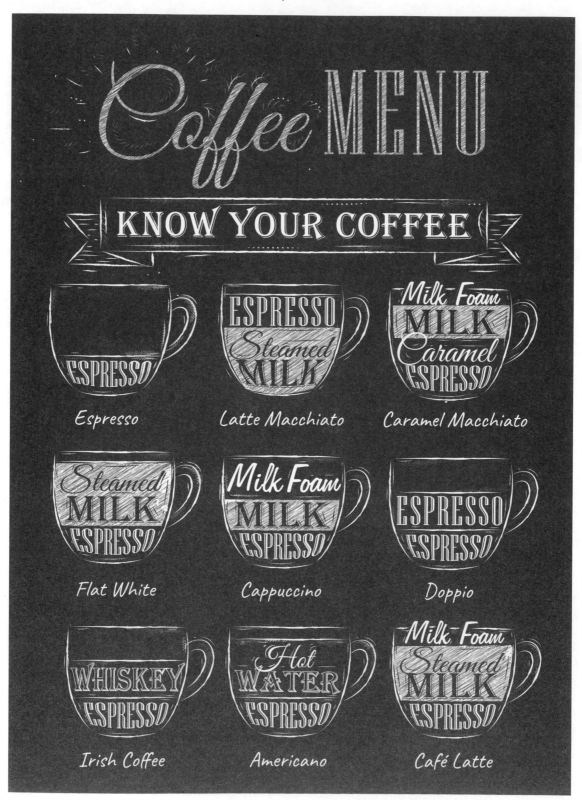

1. **What is the main difference among these coffee drinks above?**

_____

_____ 2. **According to the coffee menu above, which type of coffee drinks may a customer choose to start a day if he/she needs double the amount of a single shot Espresso?**

    (A) Irish Coffee.

    (B) Doppio.

    (C) Café Latte.

    (D) Americano.

_____ 3. **Which of the following coffee drinks is suitable for those with the inability to break down a type of natural sugar called lactose, commonly found in dairy products?**

    (A) Latte Macchiato.

    (B) Caramel Macchiato.

    (C) Cappuccino.

    (D) Americano.

4. **Describe the menu in your own words.**

_____

_____

Food & Drink

02

Read the steps and answer the questions.

Step 1

Put the ingredients for the dough into a large bowl and add 1/2 tsp salt and 125 ml warm water. Mix to a soft dough, then turn onto your work surface and knead the dough for 5 minutes or until it feels elastic. Clean and grease the bowl, and return the dough. Cover the bowl with cling film and leave it somewhere warm to rise for 1 hour, or until the dough doubled in size.

↓

Step 2

Meanwhile, make the sauce. Heat 1 tsp olive oil in a pan and add the garlic. Sizzle gently for 30 seconds, making sure the garlic doesn't brown, and then add the tomato sauce. **Season** well and bubble simmer for 8–10 minutes until you have a rich sauce—add a pinch of sugar if it tastes a little too tart. Set aside.

↓

Step 3

When the dough has risen, knock out the air and roll it into a base the same size as a large frying pan. Oil the surface of the dough, cover with cling film, and then leave it on the work surface for 15 minutes to puff up a little. Meanwhile, heat 2 tsp oil in the frying pan and add the eggplants in a single layer (you may have to cook in batches). Season well and cook for 4–5 minutes on each side until it becomes really tender and golden. Transfer to a dish and cover it with foil to keep warm.

↓

Step 4

Heat the remaining 1 tsp of oil in the pan and carefully lift the dough into it. Reshape it to fit the pan as well as possible. Cook over a low-medium heat until the underside is golden brown and the edges of the dough are starting to look dry and set—this should take about 6 minutes, but it's best to go by eye. Flip over, drizzle a little more oil around the edge of the pan so it trickles underneath the base, and cook for another 5–6 minutes until golden and cooked through. Reheat the sauce if you need to and spread it over the base. Top with the warm eggplants and dot with several spoonfuls of ricotta. Scatter with mint and drizzle with a little extra virgin olive oil just before serving.

_____ 1. **What is the purpose of this passage?**

    (A) To list the dishes that may be ordered and served.

    (B) To explain the process of how to run a restaurant.

    (C) To label the ingredients required on most packaged food.

    (D) To instruct how to make something from various ingredients.

2. **What is this passage above?**

_____

_____ 3. **The passage is written by a chef. Which kind of store might this chef serve in?**

    (A) A Thai seafood stall.

    (B) An Italian pizza house.

    (C) A Japanese sushi bar.

    (D) A Chinese cuisine restaurant.

_____ 4. **What does the word "season" mean in the second paragraph?**

    (A) To give more flavor.

    (B) To cut into pieces.

    (C) To press into a mass.

    (D) To store for one quarter of a year.

5. **Write an introductory sentence before Step 1.**

_____

Food & Drink

03

Food labels provide consumers with rich detailed food information. Understanding such information may make it easier for consumers to make quick, informed food choices that contribute to a healthy diet.

The top section of the nutrition label contains product-specific information such as the number of servings and calories. Below that, you'll find a detailed list of nutrients, including fat, sodium, carbohydrates, and more, along with their quantities and the percentage of the recommended daily intake. Read the label and answer the questions.

NUTRITION FACTS

2 servings per container
Serving size 100g

Amount per serving
Calories 547

	% Daily Value*
Total Fat 37.47g	57%
Saturated Fat 10.96g	54%
Polyunsaturated Fat 12.17g	
Monounsaturated Fat 9.84g	
Cholesterol 0mg	0%
Sodium 525mg	21%
Total Carbohydrate 49.74g	16%
Dietary Fiber 4.4g	17%
Sugar 4.12g	
Protein 6.56g	
Potassium 1,642mg	71%

* The % Daily Value (DV) tells you how much a nutrient in a serving of food contributes to a daily diet. 2,000 calories a day is used for general nutrition advice.

_____ 1. **Which of the following descriptions is correct about the food above?**

(A) One container of this food contains 547 calories.

(B) This food is with considerable amounts of salt and fat.

(C) One container of this food does not provide the necessary daily fat intake.

(D) This food contains a high proportion of protein that helps build muscle.

2. **The following figure is the Reference Daily Intake (RDI) pie chart for 4 main nutrients: fat, cholesterol, sodium, and carbohydrate. Based on the nutrition facts, what is the color that represents carbohydrate?**

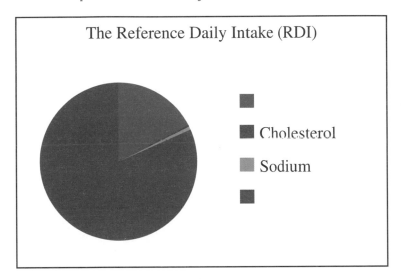

_____ 3. **Which of the following food products does the nutrition facts label above most possibly refer to?**

(A) Fruit salad.

(B) Potato chips.

(C) Watermelon juice.

(D) Tomato seafood soup.

Food & Drink

4. **Based on the following description, do you agree or disagree that it is good for people to eat this food product often?**

"Cholesterol is a compound of the sterol type found in most body tissues. Cholesterol and its derivatives are important constituents of cell membranes and precursors of other steroid compounds, but a high proportion in the blood of low-density lipoprotein (which transports cholesterol to the tissues) is associated with an increased risk of coronary heart disease.

Cholesterol comes only from animal foods. Fruits, vegetables, whole grains, and even snacks fried in vegetable oil, have no cholesterol. However, be sure to check the nutrition fact label on the food bag for saturated fat, which causes your body to produce more cholesterol. Lastly, check the serving size and do the math: if you eat 2 servings' worth, you'll need to double the calories and saturated fat."

_____

_____

_____

_____

NOTES

Read the screenshot and answer the questions.

■■■□□ SANMIN 🤝   5:54 PM   🔒 79% 🔋➔

Voted must-try in New York / Tri-State Area
March 29, 2024 at 9:25 AM

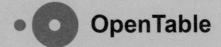

OpenTable

📍 New York / Tri-State Area (Update)

?

Stir-fry bite-sized pork with a sweet and sour sauce made of sugar, ketchup, white vinegar, and soy sauce. Additional ingredients, such as chopped pineapple, green peppers, and onions, also add an intensely pungent flavor and aroma to this dish.

Find your restaurant

_____ 1. **Which of the following pictures would be shown on this screenshot?**

(A)

(B)

(C)

(D)

2. **In which area did the customer try to find a restaurant?**

_____

_____ 3. **Which of the following nutrition facts best fits this dish?**

(A)
NUTRITION FACTS	
6 servings per dish	
Serving size	**100g**
Amount per serving	
Calories	**68**
	% Daily Value*
Total Fat 1g	**1%**
Saturated Fat 0.3g	1%
Polyunsaturated Fat 0.4g	
Cholesterol 23.2mg	**7%**
Sodium 486mg	**20%**
Total Carbohydrate 14g	**4%**
Dietary Fiber 2.6g	10%
Sugar 9.4g	
Protein 7.21g	
Potassium 1,642mg	18%

*The % Daily Value (DV) tells you how much a nutrient in a serving of food contributes to a daily diet. 2,000 calories a day is used for general nutrition advice.

(B)
NUTRITION FACTS	
6 servings per dish	
Serving size	**100g**
Amount per serving	
Calories	**183**
	% Daily Value*
Total Fat 8.2g	**12%**
Saturated Fat 2.3g	11%
Monounsaturated Fat 0.9g	
Cholesterol 0mg	**0%**
Sodium 10mg	**0%**
Total Carbohydrate 16g	**5%**
Dietary Fiber 0.4g	1%
Sugar 15g	
Protein 6.41g	
Potassium 162mg	7%

*The % Daily Value (DV) tells you how much a nutrient in a serving of food contributes to a daily diet. 2,000 calories a day is used for general nutrition advice.

Food & Drink

61

(C)

NUTRITION FACTS

6 servings per dish
Serving size   **100g**

Amount per serving	
Calories	**884**

	% Daily Value*
Total Fat 51.6g	**76%**
Saturated Fat 12.3g	**61%**
Polyunsaturated Fat 12.17g	
Monounsaturated Fat 9.84g	
Cholesterol 0mg	**0%**
Sodium 501.5mg	**20%**
Total Carbohydrate 15.4g	**5%**
Dietary Fiber 4.3g	**17%**
Sugar 12.12g	
Protein 0g	

*The % Daily Value (DV) tells you how much a nutrient in a serving of food contributes to a daily diet. 2,000 calories a day is used for general nutrition advice.

(D)

NUTRITION FACTS

6 servings per dish
Serving size   **100g**

Amount per serving	
Calories	**176**

	% Daily Value*
Total Fat 7.7g	**11%**
Saturated Fat 2.5g	**10%**
Cholesterol 24.6mg	**8%**
Sodium 520.5mg	**21%**
Total Carbohydrate 19g	**6%**
Dietary Fiber 0.3g	**1%**
Sugar 13.4g	
Protein 6.56g	

*The % Daily Value (DV) tells you how much a nutrient in a serving of food contributes to a daily diet. 2,000 calories a day is used for general nutrition advice.

4. **Based on Question 3, on what principle did you determine the nutrition facts of this dish?**

_____

_____

NOTES

Read the notice and answer the questions.

NOTICE

Catered events must be approved and scheduled before food orders are taken. Both University entities and outside community customers must contact Campus Scheduling at (208) 496–3120 to schedule on-campus events. In the case of outside community events, facility and setup charges separate from University Catering may apply. Once the event is approved by Campus Scheduling, contact University Catering to place a catered event order as far in advance as possible. Menus and service details should be finalized seven days prior to the scheduled event.

Types of Catering Service University Catering Provides:
1. Catering services for the University and outside community.
2. Delivery services to campus locations—there is no off campus delivery service.
3. Off-campus delivery on an exception basis to University approved off-campus events.
4. Takeout orders for the campus and community at large.

Late Requests / Changes:
For catered events, campus delivery, and takeout orders, there will be a late charge assessed for any late requests made with less than three business days' notice.

Cancellations:
For catered events, campus delivery, and takeout orders, there is no charge for cancellations made at least three business days prior to a scheduled event. Cancellations made less than three business days prior to an event will be subject to a service fee of 50 percent of the event total. Cancellations within one business day of the event will be charged the full amount of the event. To cancel catered events, campus delivery, and takeout orders, contact Campus Scheduling at (208) 496–3120.

Payment:
University Catering requires that each event and delivery order be prepaid six days before the scheduled event. Takeout orders are to be prepaid or paid in full at time of pickup. Any additional charges accrued the day of the event will be billed the next business day. University Catering accepts cash, checks, or Visa / Mastercard Debit / credit cards.

Sundays and Monday Nights:
University Catering does not take orders for catered events, deliveries, or takeout orders on Sundays or Monday nights after 5:00 p.m.

_____ 1. **Where may people see this notice?**

   (A) In the university academic schedule notification column.

   (B) On the university food service website.

   (C) At a local school lunch restaurant.

   (D) In the city tourism hub.

_____ 2. **Which of the following services is included in the plan?**

   (A) Online cancellation.

   (B) Twenty-four seven service.

   (C) Party decoration service.

   (D) Pick-up and local delivery.

3. **Based on the notice above, put the following steps in order.**

   (A) Free cancellation.

   (B) Finalization of menus and service detail.

   (C) Office of Event Management's approval for the scheduling catered events.

   (D) Prepaying for the event and delivery order.

   _____ → _____ → _____ → _____

4. **Based on the notice, how many evenings in a week may business orders be processed?**

   _____

06

Read the flyer and answer the questions.

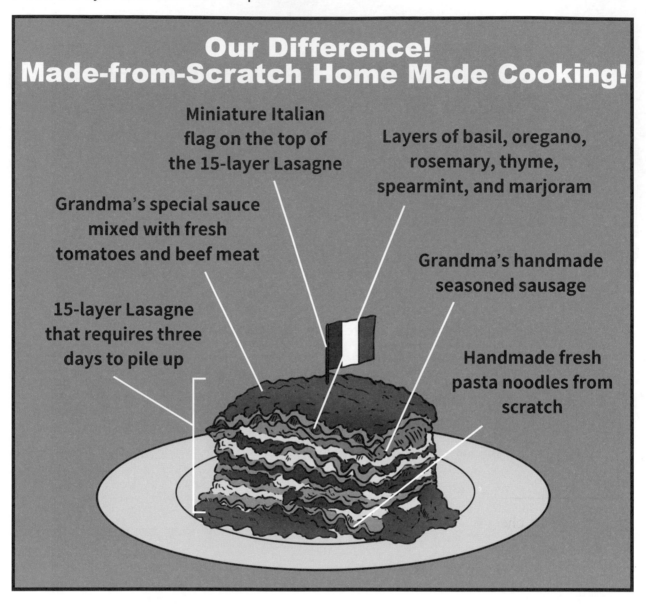

Our Difference!
Made-from-Scratch Home Made Cooking!

Miniature Italian flag on the top of the 15-layer Lasagne

Layers of basil, oregano, rosemary, thyme, spearmint, and marjoram

Grandma's special sauce mixed with fresh tomatoes and beef meat

Grandma's handmade seasoned sausage

15-layer Lasagne that requires three days to pile up

Handmade fresh pasta noodles from scratch

1. Based on the clues offered in the flyer above, what type of pasta is it?

_____

_____ 2. What is **NOT** included in this pasta dish?

(A) Sausage.

(B) Beef meat sauce.

(C) Cheddar cheese.

(D) Miniature decoration.

_____ 3. Which of the following descriptions is closest to "Made-from-Scratch" on the flyer?

(A) Providing food that has been previously prepared in factories.

(B) Having diets that involve only foods that are physically soft.

(C) Making food from the raw ingredients, rather than those that have been partially completed.

(D) Offering dishes with artificial flavors whose significant function in food is flavoring rather than nutritional.

4. According to the chef, what makes the pasta dish described above so "incredible"?

WHAT MAKES OUR INCREDIBLE LASAGNE SO INCREDIBLE?

Hi, I am Jill Wang, Executive Chef for Spaghetti Warehouse. When it comes to our spaghetti, incredible is the only word to describe it. I am not the kind of person who takes the word "incredible" lightly, but imagine our 15-layer Lasagne—a masterpiece that represents our pride in every detail. We use made-from-scratch ingredients like ricotta, Romano and mozzarella cheeses, and handmade sausage from Grandma's secret recipe of ground pork. In addition to Lasagne, our signature spaghetti flavor comes from our special sauce made from a blend of basil, oregano, rosemary, thyme, spearmint, and marjoram. I hope you will order our 15-layer Lasagne to experience the magical taste that takes us three days.

That's right, three days to prepare, and to see how we ensure every order of Lasagne is perfect every time. We believe our spaghetti will definitely surprise you with its fresh ingredients and specially-made sauce. We will try in every way to make your experience a great one here.

07

Read the menu and answer the questions.

Menu

Restaurant
Food and Drinks

Tacos	SM (small)	LG (large)
Vegetarian Taco	$1.59	$2.59
Vegetarian Soft Taco	$1.59	$2.59
Vegetarian Texas Taco	$2.69	$3.69

Quesadillas		
Spicy Rolled Quesadillas	$2.69	$3.69
Monterey Quesadillas	$3.29	$4.29
Cheese Quesadillas	$2.19	$3.19

Burritos		
Veggie Wrap	$3.49	$4.49
Vegetarian Combo	$2.99	$3.99
Red or Green	$2.29	$3.29
BRC (Beans, Rice, and Cheese)	$2.29	$3.29
Bean & Cheese	$1.59	$2.59
Tostada	$2.09	$3.09

Sandwiches		
Grilled Boca Burger	$4.39	$5.39
Vegetarian Taco Burger	$2.69	$3.69

_____ 1. **What type of food does this restaurant offer?**

(A) Stew.

(B) Fast food.

(C) Dairy products.

(D) Vegetarian meals.

_____ 2. **What categorizes the menu?**

(A) Food items.

(B) Meal prices.

(C) Calorie intake.

(D) Cooking methods.

3. **The following is the description for a certain food on the menu. What dish does it refer to?**

"It's a top choice for a hot day, either as a regular meal or a snack, depending on your preference and dietary needs. The versatile fresh vegetables and beans are gently wrapped in a home-made tortilla. The lovingly prepared roll is covered with, not one but TWO secret sauces. The tomato sauce with melted cheese gives you a sour-sweet harmony. The green chili sauce gives it a kick. Two sauces, two colors and two sensations! What are you waiting for?"

_____

4. **How much money did a customer who had originally ordered a "Bean & Cheese burrito" need to pay for extra rice?**

_____

Food & Drink

08

Read the information and answer the questions.

We Offer

Suspended Coffee

To purchase a suspended coffee, just tell the cashier what you would like to add to your order and pay. We'll serve the item to a patron in need.

To receive a suspended coffee, ask the cashier if any is available. A suspended coffee will be given on a "first come, first served" basis, without regard to race, religion, gender, etc.

This establishment reserves the right to refuse service to any patron who exhibits disruptive or disorderly conduct.

_____ 1. **What does "suspended coffee" mean?**

(A) A cup of coffee that a customer buys for others who are in need.

(B) A cup of coffee that a customer makes for the purpose of fundraising.

(C) A cup of free coffee that a boss makes for customers to celebrate the store's anniversary.

(D) A cup of fair trade coffee that supports coffee farmers around the globe in getting a fair deal.

2. Who is eligible to receive a cup of suspended coffee?

_____ 3. Which of the following slogans is suitable for the Suspended Coffee movement?

    (A) It is about more than the coffee.

    (B) Brewing justice is in your hands.

    (C) Richness worth a second cup.

    (D) From our plantation to your cup.

4. What types of people are **NOT** welcome in this activity?

Food & Drink

09

Read the chart and answer the questions.

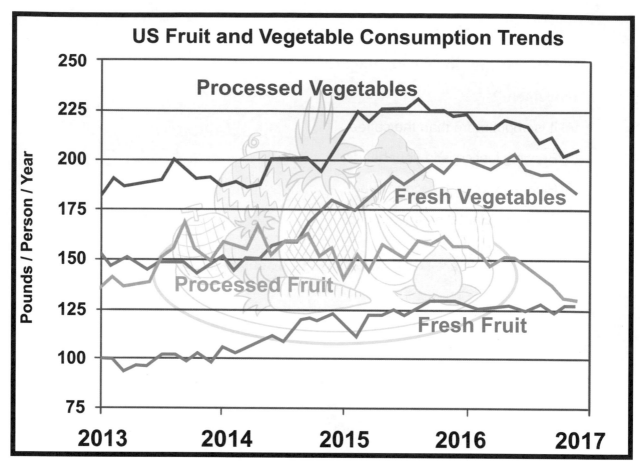

US Fruit and Vegetable Consumption Trends

Pounds / Person / Year

Processed Vegetables

Fresh Vegetables

Processed Fruit

Fresh Fruit

250 225 200 175 150 125 100 75

2013 2014 2015 2016 2017

1. **Among the four categories (processed vegetables, fresh vegetables, processed fruit, and fresh fruit), in which category was there a steady increase in consumption over the years?**

_____

2. **Based on the following analysis, explain how the US fruit and vegetable consumption habits changed.**

From the graph above, we can see that most of the decline in the produce supply has been in processed categories. There has been a decrease of about 25 pounds per person in processed vegetables (canned and frozen) due to increased knowledge of the benefits of consuming fresh produce. Moreover, the 30 pound per person drop in processed fruit consumption is mainly due to a 15 pound per person drop in orange juice consumption along with declines in canned and dried fruit consumption. By contrast, the consumption of fresh fruit and vegetables can be seen to keep increasing over recent decades. Most public health and nutrition experts would say that it would be better if Americans ate even more fresh fruit and vegetables because of their value in addressing obesity, cancer, and other health concerns, while processed foods usually contain higher amounts of salt and sugar.

_____ 3. Based on the analysis above, what caused the changes in the US fruit and vegetable consumption habits?

(A) US economic shifts.

(B) US agricultural evolution.

(C) US citizens' increasing health awareness.

(D) US health insurance system transformation.

_____ 4. If the US government would like to keep encouraging the growth of fresh fruit and vegetable consumption, which of the following strategies might be necessary?

(A) Use highly efficient, long-distance shipping methods where possible.

(B) Stimulate continued improvements in waste reduction in the production and distribution system.

(C) Encourage the local production of crops to create practical "in season" economics.

(D) Develop preservation methods such as freezing crops to maintain the taste and nutritional profiles.

Food & Drink

10

Read the picture and answer the questions.

_____ 1. **What issue does the picture try to highlight?**

    (A) Food storage and safety.

    (B) Food waste and starvation.

(C) Food poisoning and infectious organisms.

(D) Food shortage and climate change.

_____ 2. **What is the tone of the message conveyed by the picture?**

(A) Optimistic.　　　　　　　　(B) Confused.

(C) Suspicious.　　　　　　　　(D) Ironic.

3. **The following is a passage related to the picture above. Read carefully, and try to find the sentence in this passage that points out the problem developing countries are confronting.**

"Food in wealthy countries takes up only a relatively small proportion of income, so people can afford to throw food away. In developing countries, the problem is wealth, not poverty. In India's high temperatures, fruit and vegetables do not stay fresh on the market stall for long. Delhi has Asia's largest produce market and it does have a cold storage facility. But it is not big enough and rotting food is left out in piles. There is not enough investment in better farming techniques, transportation, and storage, which means lost income for small farmers and higher prices for poor consumers."

_____

_____

4. **Four people have different thoughts after reading the comic. Who do you agree most? Why?**

A: If the food was as expensive as a Ferrari, people would polish it and look after it.

B: When a man's stomach is full, it makes no difference whether he is rich or poor.

C: People want honest, flavorful food, not some showing off meals that take days to prepare.

D: There are people in the world so hungry that God cannot appear to them except in the form of bread.

_____

_____

04

大眾傳播
Mass Communication

01

The chart below is adapted from the Australian National Waste Report (2016). Study it and answer the questions.

Australia's waste producers and how much they recycle in megatons (MT)

Waste produced (MT)

Commercial & industrial | 31

Construction & demolition | 20

Household | 13.3

Waste recycled (MT)

Commercial & industrial | 17

Construction & demolition | 12

Household | 5.6

Waste landfilled (MT)

Commercial & industrial | 13

Construction & demolition | 7.1

Household | 6.5

1. According to the above chart, which kind of waste is less recycled than buried?

_____

_____ 2. Which of the following is the best title for this passage?

(A) Australia Produces a Lot of Waste, and We Are One of the Contributors

(B) Chart of the Day: Where Does Australia's Waste Come From?

(C) Restaurants, Offices, Retail, and Manufacturing—Major Polluters in Australia

(D) Who Is to Blame for Australia's Everyday Waste Production?

_____ 3. **What kind of people may find this chart useful during work?**

(A) An environment reporter.

(B) A business analyst.

(C) A sports correspondent.

(D) A software producer.

_____ 4. **Which of the following statements about the chart is NOT true?**

(A) Australian households aren't the biggest source of waste.

(B) Businesses are Australia's biggest producers of waste.

(C) 90% of the waste from construction and demolition is reused and reproduced.

(D) The waste recycled in Australia has exceeded the amount buried.

_____ 5. **What can be inferred from the chart?**

(A) Australia is running several massive construction programs at the same time.

(B) The Australian government has difficulty reducing everyday waste.

(C) Australian households have some catching up to do in terms of recycling.

(D) Australians are the biggest waste producers in the world.

02

Read the poster below and answer the questions.

We Need a 'Fair-Trade' T-shirt

Clothing industry starts with the textile industry via fashion industry to fashion retailers.

| Textile Industry | Apparel Industry | Retail Industry |

Traditional functions:

| Raw material development, production, and supply | Garment design to wholesale distribution | Distribution to the end consumer |

The Unhappy Equation of Most Kids' Clothes

 Cotton is frowning at pesticides that damage ecosystems and poison farmers. Child labor is used to keep costs down.

\+

 Cotton farmers are paid a globally set price. They are too poor to make other investments, thus trapped in a cycle of poverty.

\+

 Raw cotton is processed using poisonous heavy metals that are discharged untreated into local waterways. Harmful residues remain in the final fabric.

\+

 The garment workers, mainly women and sometimes children, work long hours in unsafe conditions. They have no rights to fight for improved pay, not to mention education.

=

 Kids' clothes are sold at a very high price.

_____ 1. **What is the purpose of this poster?**

(A) To call for fair trade in the clothing supply chain.

(B) To show how much consumers should pay for kids' clothes.

(C) To introduce how clothes are processed and sold.

(D) To explain why T-shirts can be sold at a low price.

_____ 2. **According to the poster, which of the following statements is NOT true?**

(A) Children are employed to lower the cost of producing garments.

(B) Garment workers are mostly made up of women and the uneducated.

(C) Water pollution is often caused during garment processing.

(D) The fabric that consumers finally receive is absolutely chemical free.

_____ 3. **Who might feel like protesting against the clothing industry after seeing this poster?**

(A) The textile industry.　　　　(B) Garment designers.

(C) Clothes retailers.　　　　　(D) Cotton farmers.

_____ 4. **What can be inferred from the poster?**

(A) More and more consumers are starting to care about how garments are made.

(B) The garments we wear are made by producers who exploit their workers.

(C) Artificial cotton is used in garments on the market, and it is an open secret.

(D) Clothes can be sold at a high price because the price of materials goes up.

5. **According to the poster, how does the clothing industry affect the environment?**

_____

_____

03

The following information is adapted from a website introducing a corporation named SANMIN. Read it and answer the questions below.

SANMIN has always taken pride in operational excellence and leadership in the aluminum industry since our foundation in 1880. We manufacture different kinds of high-quality aluminum products. Because of our constant innovation and maintenance of product quality, we have flourished while other companies in the traditional metal industries have declined. Now SANMIN is making every effort to minimize our impact on the environment and maximize our sustainable value to fulfill our corporate social responsibility (CSR). With the belief to be an operationally excellent as well as ethical corporation, SANMIN never stops seeking ways to be more productive and innovative. Meanwhile, we will continue to make our manufacturing eco-friendly to help contribute to sustainability.

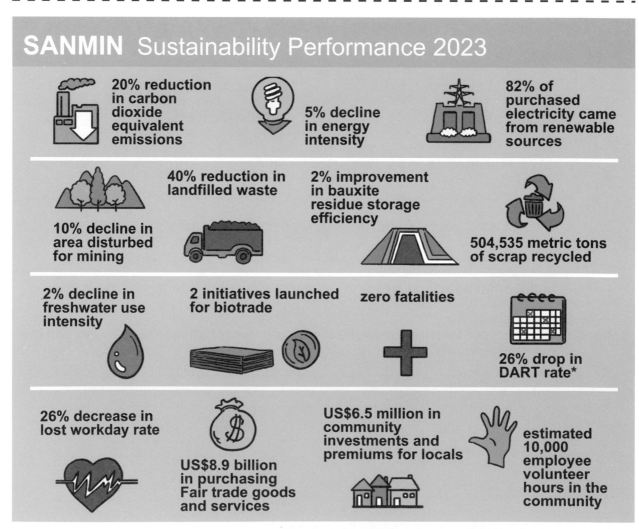

SANMIN Sustainability Performance 2023

20% reduction in carbon dioxide equivalent emissions

5% decline in energy intensity

82% of purchased electricity came from renewable sources

10% decline in area disturbed for mining

40% reduction in landfilled waste

2% improvement in bauxite residue storage efficiency

504,535 metric tons of scrap recycled

2% decline in freshwater use intensity

2 initiatives launched for biotrade

zero fatalities

26% drop in DART rate*

26% decrease in lost workday rate

US$8.9 billion in purchasing Fair trade goods and services

US$6.5 million in community investments and premiums for locals

estimated 10,000 employee volunteer hours in the community

*DART rate refers to the number of recordable injuries and illnesses per 100 full-time employees that resulted in days away from work, restricted work activity, and/or job transfers that a company has experienced in any given time frame.

_____ 1. Which of the following can best describe the passage?

    (A) SANMIN is a leading company that produces metal products.

    (B) SANMIN works hard to survive the decline of traditional industry.

    (C) SANMIN spares no effort to maintain sustainable development.

    (D) SANMIN has developed into a profitable business over the years.

_____ 2. How does SANMIN present its CSR for sustainability performance?

    (A) By giving statistics.

    (B) By telling the company's history.

    (C) By giving their customers premiums.

    (D) By rewarding their shareholders.

_____ 3. According to the 2023 sustainability performance chart shown by SANMIN, which of the following is **NOT** involved when the company develops sustainability?

    (A) The welfare of employees.

    (B) Collaborations with communities.

    (C) The discovery of renewable energy.

    (D) Investments in fair trade and biotrade.

_____ 4. Who of the following would be **LEAST** likely to be interested in this passage?

    (A) Those who campaign for environmental sustainability.

    (B) Reporters who specialize in revealing company scandals.

    (C) Activists who are deeply concerned with environmentalism.

    (D) Shareholders who value the image of the company.

5. Why does SANMIN show its sustainability performance in 2023 with a figure?

_____

_____

04

Read the two figures below and answer the questions.

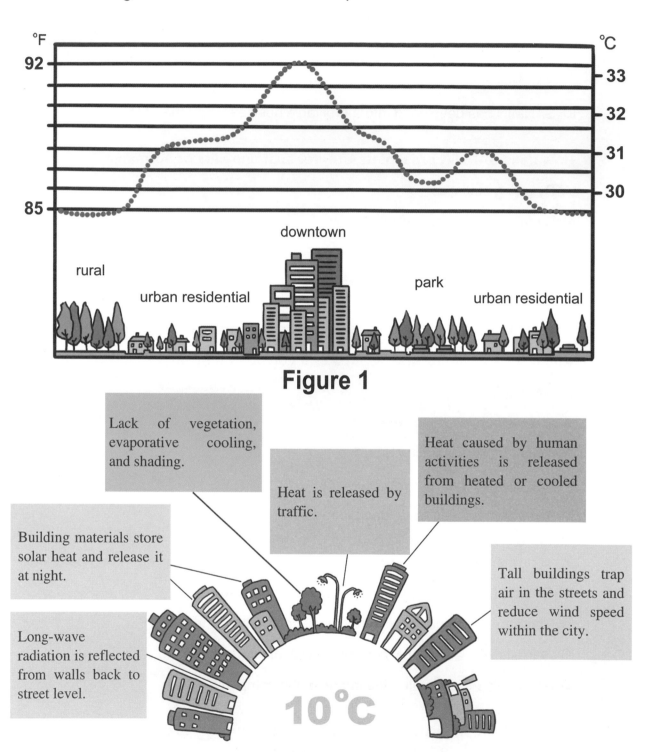

°F
92
85

°C
33
32
31
30

downtown
rural
urban residential
park
urban residential

Figure 1

Lack of vegetation, evaporative cooling, and shading.

Heat is released by traffic.

Heat caused by human activities is released from heated or cooled buildings.

Building materials store solar heat and release it at night.

Tall buildings trap air in the streets and reduce wind speed within the city.

Long-wave radiation is reflected from walls back to street level.

10°C

Because of the Urban Heat Island (UHI) effect, a city center can be over 10 degrees warmer than the surrounding countryside.

Figure 2

1. An Urban Heat Island (UHI) is a phenomenon that occurs when the downtown of a city is warmer than its surrounding countryside. List three reasons why it happens.

_____

_____

_____ 2. Joanne went to a conference this morning, and the speaker used these two figures in his talk. Which of the following might be the main title of his speech?

　(A) Unnatural Heat Caused by Human Activity

　(B) The Disasters Resulting from Heat Waves

　(C) The Harmful Effects of Climate Change in Recent Years

　(D) How Important Vegetation Distribution Is

_____ 3. According to the passage, which of the following about the UHI effect is true?

　(A) It happens not only in urban areas but also in rural areas.

　(B) It is mainly related to tall buildings in the city.

　(C) It results in higher temperatures in the countryside.

　(D) It is a phenomenon that occurs when heat is trapped in downtown areas.

_____ 4. In Figure 1, why is the temperature in the park lower than that in urban residential areas?

　(A) Trees can help increase wind speed and evaporation.

　(B) There is no long-wave radiation in green areas.

　(C) Vegetation helps reduce heat and offers shading.

　(D) The color green can absorb heat from the city.

_____ 5. Which of the following CANNOT help reduce the impact of the UHI effect?

　(A) Taking public transportation to school or work.

　(B) Building huge houses and painting them all green.

　(C) Conserving energy and reducing carbon emissions.

　(D) Reducing urban development and planting more trees.

Mass Communication

85

05

Metamorphosis is a huge transformation or change in the form of an insect or other kinds of creatures. The picture below is a brief explanation of metamorphosis. Read the picture and answer the questions.

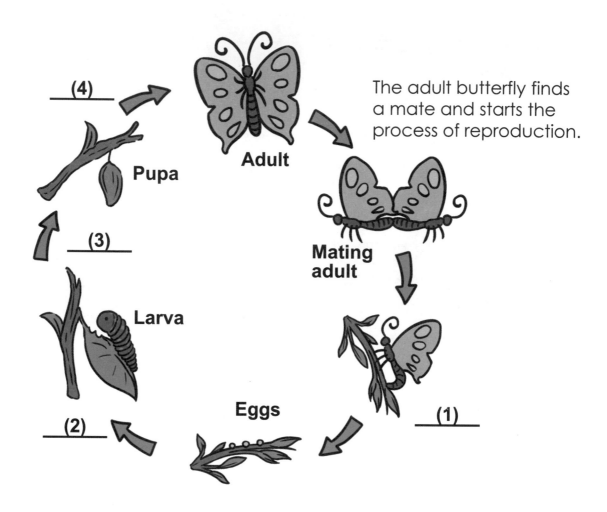

The adult butterfly finds a mate and starts the process of reproduction.

(A) A caterpillar, called a larva, hatches from an egg.

(B) In the pupa stage, the larva undergoes metamorphosis.

(C) Adult butterflies lay their eggs on the leaves.

(D) The larva hangs itself upside down, with its body shortening and thickening until it forms a hard case called a cocoon around itself.

1. **Put the statements A to D in the correct order of the life cycle of a butterfly.**

   Ans: (1)_____ ⇒ (2)_____ ⇒ (3)_____ ⇒ (4)_____

_____ 2. **According to the given information, which of the following statements is true?**

   (A) Metamorphosis occurs in small insects only.

   (B) Caterpillars are delicate after being hatched.

   (C) Butterflies start reproduction in the pupa stage.

   (D) A cocoon is a case made to cover an insect.

Read the passage below and answer the questions.

> A man found a small opening on a butterfly's cocoon. He watched the butterfly inside struggle to force its body through that little hole. Kind and eager to help, he cut off the remaining part of the cocoon with a pair of scissors. The butterfly then came out easily, but it had a swollen body and small wings. The man expected that the wings would expand so that it could start its new journey in the sky. However, it didn't happen. The butterfly spent the rest of its life crawling on the ground and couldn't fly like the others of its species.

_____ 3. **What happened to the butterfly in the passage?**

   (A) It became crippled because its wing was cut by the man.

   (B) It became very energetic after coming out of the cocoon.

   (C) It didn't go through the necessary struggle to get out of the cocoon.

   (D) It didn't undergo the metamorphosis to become an adult butterfly.

4. **What is the message behind the passage?**

   _____

   _____

06

Confronting Trash Talk in Your Work Team

Originally published on April 20, 2023 at 2:00 p.m.

By Eliz Leyn

Q: One of my team members quit, and somehow I knew she was trash-talking me in front of other team members. Now I have trouble trusting the members and their loyalty. How can I cope with it?

> Kenny, 48, head of a team at a high-tech company

A: It is definitely a waste of time to think too much about a coworker who has been trash-talking you, especially if that person has already quit. Stop discouraging yourself anymore, though it is indeed frustrating to be misunderstood. I suggest that you focus on the brighter side and think about your team members' positive characteristics. Separating your thoughts from this incident will help your move on. However, if the uncomfortable situation continues, you'll need to confront the **perpetrator** to end it! Prepare carefully for the conversation with that person. Stay calm and don't rush it while having the talk. Just keep in mind that you should never do anything that will have a destructive influence on the team. Don't worry too much about the consequences. At least you are willing to make changes. There is nothing worse than feedback that never gets acted on. Last but not least, **trust and loyalty are a two-way street**. It's naïve to think that your team will be loyal to you unless you have set up an environment that is mutually supportive.

Eliz Leyn: eliz@coachingandconsulting.com.
Eliz Leyn is a qualified coach with more than
20 years of business experience.

_____ 1. **What can we know about this passage?**

(A) It is a comment on a trending online news article.

(B) It is a marketing project from Kenny's company.

(C) It is a psychological column about workplace relations.

(D) It is a book review of Eliz Leyn's new publication.

_____ 2. **Why did Kenny seek advice from Eliz Leyn?**

(A) Kenny couldn't endure any trash talk from his colleagues.

(B) Kenny was angry that his colleagues got the promotion.

(C) Kenny had no idea how to deal with his former coworker's behavior.

(D) Kenny tried to find some aggressive ways to respond to his colleagues.

_____ 3. **After reading the passage, which of the following is Leyn's suggestion for Kenny?**

(A) She suggested that Kenny dismiss his team and clear up misunderstandings.

(B) She recommended that Kenny talk to each of his teammates.

(C) She advised Kenny to stand in the shoes of the departed staff member.

(D) She guided Kenny to be objective and focus on incidents rather than people.

_____ 4. **What does the underlined word "perpetrator" refer to?**

(A) The negative feedback that Kenny was faced with.

(B) The person who did terrible things to Kenny.

(C) The person who used accusatory-based language.

(D) The fact that Kenny was scolded by his colleagues.

5. **Why did Eliz Leyn mention "trust and loyalty are a two-way street"? What did she imply to Kenny?**

_____

_____

07

The following two paragraphs are excerpted from the same journal paper. Read the extracts and answer the questions.

The ways we travel make a big difference in the emissions of CO_2 and other greenhouse gases, which cause climate change. Transportation accounts for approximately 24% of total CO_2 emissions, 90% of which is attributed to road transport. The type of vehicle and its load determine the amount of CO_2 emitted per passenger and kilometer. As the chart below (Figure 1) shows, biking puts **negligible** CO_2 into the air, while driving a private car produces the most significant levels of CO_2 emissions per passenger and kilometer. Though traveling by public transport is always encouraged to help reduce carbon emissions, each bus passenger emits an average of 161 grams of CO_2 per kilometer. The continual improvement of public transport is required.

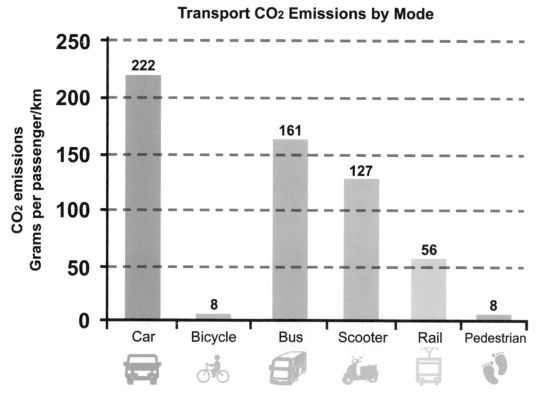

Transport CO₂ Emissions by Mode

* The figure for Bus is based on average occupancy on a national level.

Figure 1

There has been a reduction in fuel consumption since 2014, which has further contributed to the drop in greenhouse gas emissions (Figure 2). This decrease is mainly credited to the improvement of public transportation. Nearly 96% of the bus companies are now funded to buy electric vehicles.

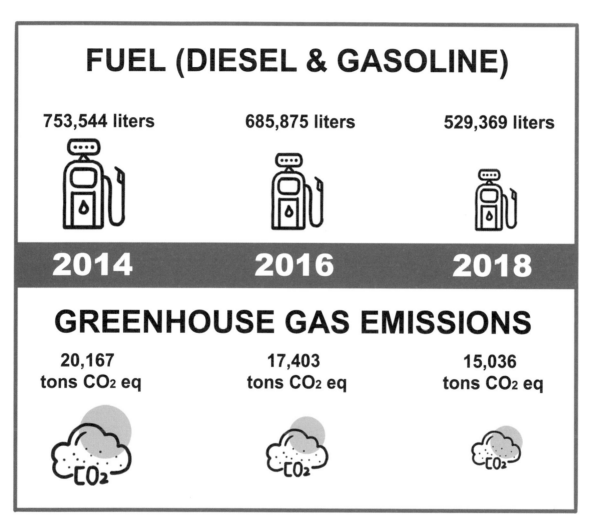

Figure 2

1. According to Figure 1, which two of the transport modes are the most environmentally friendly?

_____ and _____ .

_____ 2. According to the above two excerpts, what issue is this journal paper **LEAST** likely to address?

(A) Reasons for the decrease in greenhouse gas emissions since 2014.

(B) The effects different modes of travel have on total emissions.

(C) How greenhouse gas emissions make climate change worse.

(D) The role fuel plays in reducing the amount of greenhouse gases.

_____ 3. Which of the following is closest in meaning to the underlined word "negligible" in the first passage?

(A) So small and not worth considering.

(B) Too important to be ignored.

(C) More noticeable than the others.

(D) Harmful and dangerous to humans.

_____ 4. Which of the following best describes the information in the two excerpts?

(A) The best solution for urban transport problems is to have all pedestrians ride bicycles.

(B) The increase in the number of carpooling accounts for the decrease in emissions since 2014.

(C) Varying the modes of public transportation in a city will cause higher fuel prices.

(D) Electric vehicles play a crucial role in helping reduce greenhouse gas emissions.

NOTES

08

Have you ever heard of a "bomb cyclone"? Some people say it is an exaggeration to describe a weather phenomenon, but there is actually a stringent set of criteria behind the classification of a storm as a "weather bomb" or an "explosive storm." Look at the picture and read the text below to find out how a weather anchor defines bombogenesis.

A "Bomb Cyclone" occurs when a developing storm rapidly intensifies with the pressure dropping more than 24 millibars (mb) in 24 hours.

We all know that the air pressure of a cyclone determines how strong the storm may be. The lower the pressure, the stronger the storm. Typically, the surface air pressure of a storm tends to be 1010 millibars, and most of the big storms that sweep across the United States are around 995 or 990. But for a storm to be defined as a "bomb," it has to drop at least 24 millibars in 24 hours.

Many bomb cyclones are accompanied by heavy rain or locally heavy snow, coastal flooding, and hurricane-force wind gusts. Recently, winter storms have made the entire East Coast unusually cold, turning the eastern United States into a whiteout world. According to statistics, while the world is actually 0.5 degrees Celsius warmer than average this winter, Canada and the U.S. are currently the most abnormally cold places on Earth. Clearly, with such strange weather patterns occurring, the climate will only become more unpredictable.

_____ 1. What is the passage mainly about?

(A) A new-found weapon.

(B) A political report.

(C) A weather phenomenon.

(D) A disaster prediction.

_____ 2. Which of the following is **NOT** one of the requirements for forming a bomb cyclone?

(A) It must be a low-pressure system.

(B) The storm strengthens rapidly.

(C) Its pressure drops ≥ 24 mb in 24 hours.

(D) It must be accompanied by a hurricane.

_____ 3. When a bomb cyclone strikes, which of the following will **NOT** take place?

(A)

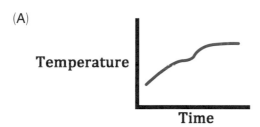

(B)

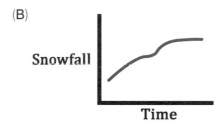

(C)

Blizzard

(D)

Flood

_____ 4. What is most likely to be discussed in the next paragraph?

(A) How to precisely predict bomb cyclones.

(B) The reason causes extreme weather these years.

(C) The time the next bomb cyclone sweeps across the United States.

(D) Whether the total snowfall in the eastern America will break the records.

5. After reading this passage, do you agree with some people's comments that it is an exaggeration to describe this weather phenomenon as a "bomb cyclone"? Why or why not?

09

Read the information below and answer the questions.

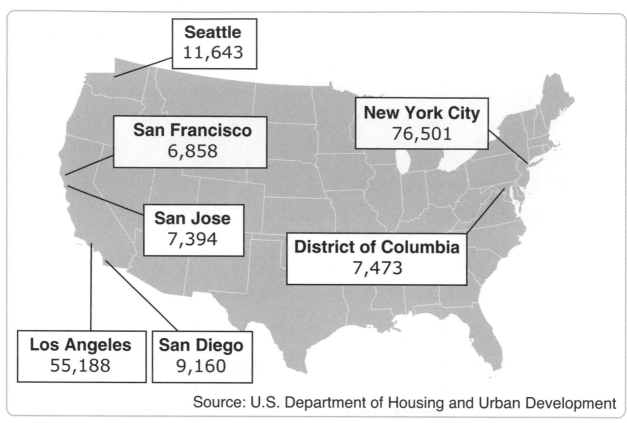

Seattle
11,643

New York City
76,501

San Francisco
6,858

San Jose
7,394

District of Columbia
7,473

Los Angeles
55,188

San Diego
9,160

Source: U.S. Department of Housing and Urban Development

Top 7 Cities with Most Homeless Population in 2017

_____ 1. **Which information CANNOT be found in the figure above?**

(A) The total number of homeless Americans in 2017.

(B) The rankings of cities in the U.S. for homeless populations.

(C) The distribution of homeless people across the United States.

(D) The division of the government that makes up this map chart.

_____ 2. **Which of the following statements is true?**

(A) New York City has had the highest number of homeless people for years.

(B) The homeless population in San Jose is only exceeded by District of Columbia.

(C) Los Angeles had the second-largest homeless population in 2017.

(D) San Francisco had the smallest homeless population in the States in 2017.

"... The number of homeless continues to trend upward. Since 2007, the estimated number of people without permanent shelter has risen by 47 percent, leaving _____ _____ ranking third in the number of not only the homeless population but also the unsheltered homeless—those living in vehicles, tents, and on local streets. The 5,485 unsheltered people counted in the county in 2017 represent a 21 percent increase over last year's tally."

3. The above description is cited from a local newspaper in the U.S. According to the above figure and the passage, which city is the best to fit in the blank?

_____

_____ 4. Which is the most likely chart to account for the phenomenon in the above description?

(A)

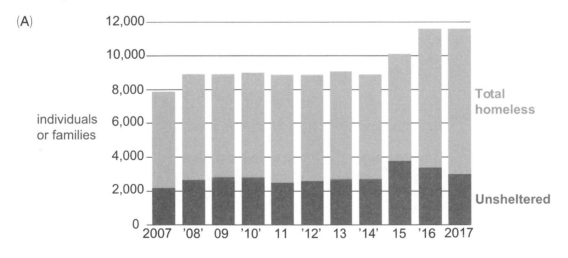

(B)

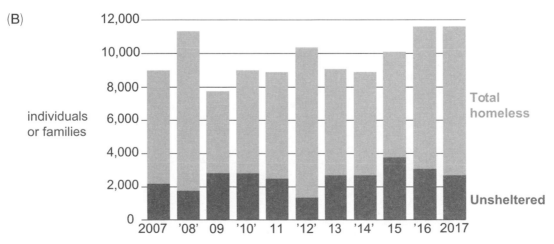

(C)

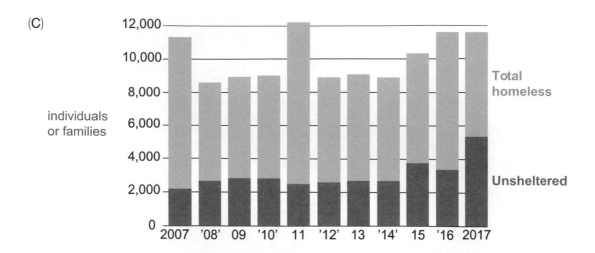

(D)

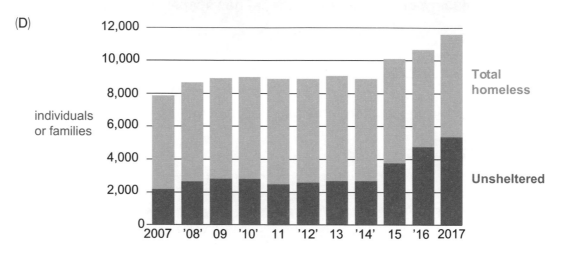

NOTES

活用英文：實用英文閱讀訓練

10

The description below is the first paragraph of a geography news article. Answer the questions after reading the passage and studying the two figures.

The Rattlesnake Hills are 3 miles south of Yakima, WA. Recently, a landslide has been observed occurring above the north of a **quarry**, bounded by Thorp Rd. to the south and west. About 20 acres of land within the Rattlesnake Hills are moving at a rate of 1.6 ft/week in a southward direction. This type of collapse is a translational landslide, consisting of blocks of basalt sliding on a weaker sedimentary layer. Experts suggest that the landslide will most likely move into the quarry, affecting Thorp Rd. The worst case is that it could hit highway I-82 and impact homes south of the quarry, or potentially run out beyond I-82 and reach the Yakima River.

Figure 1

Figure 2

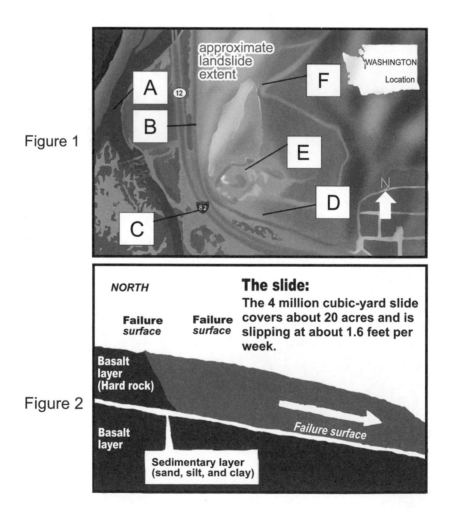

1. Read Figure 1. In which location (A to F) can we find the "quarry" mentioned in the passage?

_____ 2. According to the description above, which location in Figure 1 is **LEAST** likely to be affected once the landslide takes place?

(A) A　　　　　(B) B　　　　　(C) D　　　　　(D) F

_____ 3. Which of the following topics might be discussed in the next paragraph of this article?

(A) Precautions to be taken for the landslide.

(B) Factors that cause the flooding downriver.

(C) The ecosystem around the Rattlesnake Hills.

(D) The relationship between the quarry and the Yakima River.

_____ 4. Which word is closest in meaning to the word "failure" in Figure 2?

(A) Block.　　　(B) Collapse.　　　(C) Quarry.　　　(D) Scenario.

NOTES

核心英文字彙力
2001～4500(三版)

丁雍嫻　邢雯桂
盧思嘉　應惠蕙　編著

◆ **最新字表！**

依據大學入學考試中心公布之「高中英文參考詞彙表 (111 學年度起適用)」
編寫，一起迎戰 108 新課綱。單字比對歷屆試題，依字頻平均分散各回。

◆ **符合學測範圍！**

收錄 Level 3~5 學測必備單字，規劃 100 回。聚焦關鍵核心字彙、備戰學測。
Level 3：40 回
Level 4：40 回
Level 5-1(精選 Level 5 高頻單字)：20 回

◆ **素養例句！**

精心撰寫各式情境例句，符合 108 新課綱素養精神。除了可以利用例句學習
單字用法、加深單字記憶，更能熟悉學測常見情境、為大考做好準備。

◆ **補充詳盡！**

常用搭配詞、介系詞、同反義字及片語等各項補充豐富，一起舉一反三、輕
鬆延伸學習範圍。

WORD UP 數位學習特惠販售中

英文作文
這樣寫，就 OK

提升你的英文寫作能力，
這一本就 OK ！

張淑娛、應惠蕙　編著／車昀庭　審定

1. 從「中英文句子基本結構的差異」、「腦力激盪」的概念談起，引導你從基礎寫作開始練習。
2. 介紹常見的英文文體，包括敘述文、描寫文、看圖寫作、說明文、書信寫作、圖表寫作與議論文，讓你充分學習每一種文體的寫作技巧。
3. 提點寫作重點與步驟，替你打下扎實的寫作基本功。
4. 補充圖表寫作的寫作技巧，符合新課綱核心素養導向，讓你先會先贏。
5. 內容豐富充實，按部就班練習，自學、教學一本就 OK ！

國家圖書館出版品預行編目資料

活用英文：實用英文閱讀訓練 Effective English: Skills
for Practical Reading Comprehension／王信雲,李秋芸
編著.－－修訂二版一刷.－－臺北市：三民，2024
　　　面；　　公分.－－（Reading Power系列）

　　ISBN 978-957-14-7742-8　（平裝）
　　1. 英語 2. 讀本

805.18　　　　　　　　　　　　　　112021513

 Reading Power 系列

活用英文：實用英文閱讀訓練
Effective English: Skills for Practical Reading Comprehension

編 著 者	王信雲　李秋芸
責任編輯	洪愷澤　蔡品維
美術編輯	康智瑄
內頁繪圖	陳則旻

發 行 人	劉振強
出 版 者	三民書局股份有限公司
地　　址	臺北市復興北路 386 號 (復北門市)
	臺北市重慶南路一段 61 號 (重南門市)
電　　話	(02)25006600
網　　址	三民網路書店 https://www.sanmin.com.tw

出版日期	初版一刷 2019 年 1 月
	修訂二版一刷 2024 年 1 月
書籍編號	S807310
I S B N	978-957-14-7742-8

三民書局

★ 108 課綱、全民英檢中級／中高級、
TOEIC 新多益英語測驗適用
★ 可搭配 108 課綱選修課程

Intermediate

Effective English:
Skills for Practical Reading Comprehension

活用英文：

實用英文閱讀訓練

解析本

王信雲、李秋芸 編著　　Ian Fletcher 審定

三民書局

Travel & Transportation

Unit 1

1. C　2. C　3. C　4. A
5. Though the density of the cars has increased, that of the scooters has decreased more, which leads to the overall decreased density of motor vehicles.

本篇為名片 (business card)。名片上有姓名、服務機構、職稱與連絡方式 (地址與電話)。

1. Teuber 先生在哪裡工作？
   (A) 在公車站。
   (B) 在警察局。
   (C) 在政府部門辦公室。
   (D) 在工程公司。
   　由名片中的 Sanmin City、Transportation Department 和 Traffic Control and Engineering Division 等資訊可知，Teuber 先生在三民市政府交通處的交通控制與工程組工作，故正確答案為(C)。

2. 以下何者可能是 Teuber 先生的工作職責？
   (A) 販賣車輛。
   (B) 修理車輛。
   (C) 執行交通政策。
   (D) 用季節性裝飾品美化城市。
   　由名片中 Teuber 先生職稱下方的 Maintaining high standards in traffic control and engineering for the city transportation 可知他的工作內容為維護高標準的交通管制和城市交通工程，雖有 traffic 和 transportation 字樣，但指的是交通，而非個別車輛，且也無與販賣、修理相關的詞彙。另外，由於 Teuber 先生的工作為交通工程相關，與(D)的美化城市無關，故選(C)。

3. 以下何者不是此卡片的功能？
   (A) 介紹 Teuber 先生。
   (B) 指出 Teuber 先生的工作專長。
   (C) 提醒別人 Teuber 先生的電子郵件。
   (D) 告知別人 Teuber 先生的辦公室地址。

名片功能為向對方介紹自己。Teuber 先生的名片下方有註明辦公室地址、電話與他的工作職稱，由職稱可以知道 Teuber 先生的工作專長，而此名片中並未提供電子郵件，故(C)為正確答案。

4. 以下表格為關於三民市車輛數量與密度的資訊。下列哪一資訊無法於此表找到？
   (A) 歷年使用者密度的變化。
   (B) 車輛與機車的比例。
   (C) 車輛數量的增加。
   (D) 機車密度的減少。
   　此表能呈現汽機車數量和密度的變化，但並無呈現汽機車使用者的資訊。且由於一人可能擁有多臺汽機車，以此數據無法推論出使用者數量和密度，故選(A)。
   (B)將車輛數量除以機車數量即得汽機車比例。

5. 根據以上表格，就車輛密度越來越高，但整體汽機車密度卻降低之現象做出可能的解釋。
   由以上表格，我們可看到汽車密度雖逐年升高，但機車密度卻降低，且後者降低幅度比前者升高幅度大，因此導致整體汽機車密度降低。

1

Unit 2

1. B　2. C　3. D
4. Based on the regulation explanation above, the lady faced a penalty fine because, though she was a mother, she did not take her kid(s) with her.

本篇為停車場管理告示。在上面可以觀察到該停車場的各種停車規定，包括罰金的金額與使用者應遵守的規則。

1. 人們可以在何處看到此告示牌？
   (A) 在市政府附近的停車區。
   (B) 在購物中心的停車場。
   (C) 在住宅的停車場。
   (D) 在中學的停車場。

   告示牌上寫有 Customer Only 字樣，表示該地應有進行商業活動，(A)、(C)、(D)三地皆不是進行商業活動的地方，應不會使用顧客一詞，且從標題的 Sanmin Outlet 亦可知此地應是購物中心的停車場，故選(B)。

2. 下列哪種情況不會導致停車罰款？
   (A) 在一小時內再次進入。
   (B) 停親子車位卻無孩童陪同。
   (C) 在特定區域停車。
   (D) 停在殘障車位但車上沒有殘障標示。

   由「No return within 2 hours」得知，在出停車場後的兩小時內再進場即會被罰款；由「The driver must be accompanied by a child.」得知，有小孩陪同的父母才有停親子停車位的權益；由「Disabled bays are for disabled badge holders only」得知殘障停車位僅提供給持有殘障徽章的人使用。由「Parking only within marked bays」得知將車停在特定區域就不會收到罰款，故(C)為正確選項。

3. 一位女士帶著兩位兒童進入了此停車場，她應該將車停在哪裡？
   (A) 在貴賓停車區。
   (B) 在殘障停車格。
   (C) 在無保全巡邏的停車場。
   (D) 在有標記的停車位。

管理須知並無標示貴賓停車區；攜帶著孩子與殘障停車的資格無關；由「This parking lot is patrolled.」可知全停車場皆為保全巡邏區域。告示牌上的「Parent & child parking only within marked bays」字樣，即指出帶著孩子的父母可以將車停入有專屬標示的格線中，故(D)為正確選項。

4. 根據以下的情況，為何那位女士須面對罰款？

此文章的第一段點出，停車在親子車位的車主，若沒有 12 歲以下的小孩在身邊，就不可使用此停車位，否則將會開罰。此文章的第二段則更清楚說明這位女士的確是因為未依循親子車位的使用方法而被開罰。

Unit 3

1. B　　2. D　　3. D
4. The phrase "or part thereof" refers not just to the entire period of time, but to any smaller part of it as well. In this case, "first 3 hours or part thereof" means even if you park for less than 3 hours, you'll still have to pay for 3 hours.

本篇為停車場費率告示。閱讀時應注意在各時段停車的不同費率，以及除一般停車外可能產生的額外費用與各項相關規定。

1. 在週間，最少停車幾小時會讓駕駛得繳最高額的停車費？
   (A) 15 小時。
   (B) 12 小時。
   (C) 9 小時。
   (D) 6 小時。

   週間的停車費上限為 600 元，這段時間停車前三小時收費為固定 150 元，之後每一小時以 50 元計。首先將 600 元減掉前三小時的 150 元後為 450 元，將之除以每小時收費 50 元後可得 9 小時，9 小時再加上固定費率的三小時即為 12 小時，故選(B)。

2. 在 12 月 24 日，王家為了耶誕節去採購，車停了 4 小時。當他們要準備離開時，才發現他們的停車票卡遺失了。他們需要付多少錢？
   (A) 400 元。
   (B) 1,000 元。
   (C) 1,400 元。
   (D) 1,500 元。

   假日收費標準為前兩小時固定 300 元，之後每半小時 50 元，因此計算方式為 300 元加上後面兩小時的 200 元，共 500 元。除此之外，遺失票卡必須額外付 1,000 元，因此總共應付(D) 1,500 元。

3. 1 月 1 日凌晨 1 點，保全人員在停車場發現一輛停過夜的車輛。透過監視器，他注意到這部車在前一天晚上 6 點進入停車場。早上 6 點，一群年輕人宣稱他們為了附近的跨年派對把車子停過夜。他們總共需付多少錢？
   (A) 500 元。
   (B) 850 元。
   (C) 1,700 元。
   (D) 2,200 元。

   假日及假日前夕的收費標準為前兩小時固定 300 元，之後以每半小時 50 元計。截至 31 日 12 點前他們共停了 6 小時，費用為前兩小時的 300 元加上後面四小時的 400 元，共 700 元。而由於車主於 1 月 1 日停車場一開門即來取車，因此 1 日早上並沒有產生費用，但是他們必須付 1,500 元的過夜保管費，故總共應付 (D) 2,200 元。

4. 請問「First 3 hours or part thereof」的意思為何？請用自己的話解釋。
   片語 or part thereof 指整體當中的一部分。因此，first 3 hours or part thereof 是指前三小時，但若未滿三小時則以三小時計。

Unit 4

1. B 2. A 3. A 4. A 5. 如下圖。

本篇為道路整修公告。閱讀時應注意整修的時間、地點、整修的內容與注意事項。

1. 以下哪一條路將在施工中？

(A) A 路。 **(B) B 路。** (C) C 路。 (D) D 路。

由公告中「The City Hall will be resurfacing the roadway on King's Road from Route 236 to Park Avenue East.」得知施工區域為 King's Road 上由 Route 236 至 Park Avenue 東部區域的路段，選項中有從 Route 236 到 Park Avenue 的只有 B 路，因此得知答案為(B)。

2. 以下哪一項目未包含在此計劃內？

(A) 人行道移除。 (B) 斑馬線畫線。

(C) 草皮替換。 (D) 道路標線繪製。

由公告得知以下工程包含在此項計劃中：Repairing and resurfacing road surface (路面修理及重新鋪設)、Sidewalk and curb repairs, pavement markings, driveway restoration, and lawn replacement (人行道及路緣修理、路面標示、車道維護及草皮替換)。由此得知(A)未包含於計劃中。

3. Javier：不敢相信我忘記今天要重鋪路面。

Martina：難怪你今天這麼晚到。

Javier：對啊，我以為我可以左轉到 King's Road，然後在 King's Road 和 Forest Avenue 的交叉口右轉，但是我錯了。

Martina：所以，你怎麼來這裡的？

Javier：我得繼續再往東開 2 英里，然後向北走老遠到 Queen's Park，在那我才終於能轉到 Forest Avenue。

Martina：喔！你好可憐。

根據以上對話與公告，請問下列何者為此地圖的正確方位？

由對話可知 Javier 要左轉到 King's Road，所以他一開始可能是從 Route 236 向地圖的右邊行駛，或是從 Park Avenue 向地圖的左邊行駛。但是根據 I had to go another 2 miles east and then go a long way north to Queen's Park 可知，他沿著道路行駛後轉彎向北開到 Queen's Park，由此推論出他的原始位置是在 Route 236。最後分析他所提到的方位後即可得知地圖上方為北方，故選(A)。

4. 以下何者文意最接近公告中最後一部分的「adjacent to」？

(A) 靠近。 (B) 遙遠。 (C) 超越。 (D) 對面。

由公告最後一句 Temporary lane closures and parking restrictions adjacent to construction zones will be in effect. 可得知，會被影響到的區域應為「接近」或「靠近」施工區域的街道和停車格，故選(A)。

5. 報導指出有一間公立學校將會蓋在 King's Road、Forest Ave. 和 Main Street 所環繞的區域。在以下地圖用斜線劃記此指定區域。

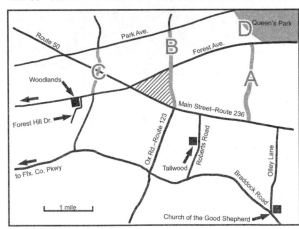

由公告中的 The City Hall will be resurfacing the roadway on King's Road from Route 236 to Park Avenue East. 得知，Road B 即是 King's Road，即施工路段。因此由 Road B、Main Street 和 Forest Ave. 所環繞的區域即如上圖所示。

Unit 5

1. B　2. C　3. D　4. A

本篇為機艙廣播。內容有坐飛機應注意的各種事項，包含各種安全設施的使用方式、緊急疏散注意事項等。

1. 旅客可能在何種交通工具聽到這則廣播？
   (A) 火車。
   (B) 飛機。
   (C) 遊覽車。
   (D) 郵輪。
   　　由 turbulence (亂流) 和 aircraft (飛機) 等字樣，可知答案為(B)。

2. 此廣播目的為何？
   (A) 起飛通知。
   (B) 月臺改變提醒。
   (C) 安全示範解釋。
   (D) 誤點資訊。
   　　由此廣播中提到「安全帶」、「逃生方向」、「氧氣面罩」和「逃生背心」資訊得知，此廣播目的為(C)。

3. 在此廣播中，以下哪一資訊未被提及？
   (A) 疏散流程。
   (B) 救生衣使用方法。
   (C) 安全帶使用方法。
   (D) 乘客保險申請。
   　　(A)、(B)、(C)在廣播中都有提到，但未提及乘客保險，故答案為(D)。

4. 此句「In the event of a decompression, an oxygen mask will automatically appear in front of you.」最適合安插在以下段落何處？
   (A) ①。
   (B) ②。
   (C) ③。
   (D) ④。
   　　此句是在解釋使用氧氣前的過程，因此最適合將此句安插於「To start the flow of oxygen, pull the mask toward you.」之前，故可知答案為(A)。

Unit 6

1. D　2. D　3. 2013.
4. Low-cost flights.

本篇為與飛航相關的統計圖。上圖為折線圖，閱讀時應注意圖的縱、橫軸，以及資訊隨時間變化的趨勢；下圖為長條狀的百分比圖，一整條為 100%，可以呈現出各部分所占之百分比。

1. 以上圖表的目的為何？
   (A) 用來呈現國家機場的噪音等量線。
   (B) 用來呈現飛機總量的穩定成長。
   (C) 用來解釋飛機平均年齡的增加。
   (D) 用來指出不同飛機系列的增加和減少。
   　　由表中的縱座標 Total flights by airline category、橫座標的年份可知，本圖要呈現不同種類航空公司航次的數量隨時間增加或減少的趨勢，故(D)為正解。

2. 根據上圖，以下描述何者正確？
   (A) 貨機數量在 2012 年和 2013 年間數量增加。
   (B) 包機航班數量最後超越其他機種。
   (C) 飛機總量在此十年間維持穩定。
   (D) 廉價航空的比例從 2005 年到 2014 年幾乎成長了一倍。
   　　上圖代表貨機的黃色曲線在 2012 年和 2013 年並無明顯上升，因此可推論數量並未增加；上圖代表包機航班的藍色曲線最後並未超越其他機種；上圖代表飛機總量的黑色曲線，在此十年中仍有明顯上升與下降，代表並不穩定。由下圖可以觀察到各種不同航空公司佔總業界的比例，2005 年以綠色代表的廉價航空佔 13.7%，2014 年則升至 27.5%，約是 2005 年的兩倍，故可知(D)選項正確。

3. 在何年所有飛機的總量達最低點？
   　　代表飛機總量的黑色曲線在 2013 年達最低點，故可知所有飛機的總量在 2013 年達最低點。

4. 哪種機種的數量在 2012 年經歷了微幅的增長？

從 2011 年到 2012 年，其他機種的顏色曲線皆呈現下降的趨勢，只有代表廉價航空的綠色曲線微幅上升，故答案為廉價航空 (Low-cost flights)。

Unit 7

1. A　2. Bantry.　3. 3　4. D

本篇為交通工具時間表。要注意班次的時間與旺、淡季的班次安排，以及特殊的班次安排。

1. 根據以上時間表，請問此搭載乘客的交通工具種類為何？

   (A) 渡輪。

   (B) 火車。

   (C) 遊覽車。

   (D) 飛機。

   由時間表上的 Harbor Cruises (港口遊覽) 字樣可得知正解為(A)。

2. 現在是 7 月，Mason 在這星期六要參加一個在港口附近的派對。他打算在下午 5 點 50 分離開派對，前往港口搭乘交通工具。他可能要去哪個港口？

   由時間表可以看出 Whiddy 在 7 月星期六的最後一趟船班是下午 5 點 45 分發船，若 Mason 在 5 點 50 分才離開派對，是趕不上船班的；而 Bantry 的最後一趟船班是 6 點發船，Mason 在 5 點 50 分離開派對是有可能趕上船班的，由此可知他應該是前往 Bantry 搭船。

3. 在淡季期間 (9 月至 5 月)，一天至少提供幾趟旅程？

   因題目詢問冬天淡季，故應查看 9 月至 5 月的欄位。且因題目詢問「至少」提供幾趟旅程，故查看最少次的出發時間，即為三趟。

4. Sharmila 正邀請朋友參加這星期天的夜晚港口遊覽。在邀請函上，她應該寫什麼時間來提醒賓客準時上船？

   (A) 8:55。

   (B) 11:55。

   (C) 15:55。

   (D) 18:55。

   由傳單上的 Evening cruise 19:00 by arrangement 與最後的 Please get on board 5 mins before departure. 可知應選(D) 18:55。

Unit 8

1. To explain why Ms. Wang paid less than the original fare and to inform her that she would not be charged the original fare. In addition, the electronic tickets and itinerary receipt have been sent to her.
2. D 3. C 4. D 5. A

本篇為客戶服務的電子郵件。應注意寄件人和收件人的姓名與職稱等個人訊息，以判斷兩人的關係，再閱讀信件主題，了解此信件的訊息。

1. 此封郵件的目的為何？

由此信中第一段 we have investigated the concerns which you raised with regards to your booking for the cruise vacation to Maldives. (我們已對您所提出馬爾地夫郵輪的訂票事宜做出調查) 得知，此信目的是向對方釋疑。而由信中第二段 we will honor the booking which you made. Please be informed that we have sent the electronic tickets and the itinerary receipt to you. (我們將會接受您的預訂。請注意，我們已寄出電子票券和收據給您。) 得知此描述為解決方法。

2. 請問 Michael 可能在哪間公司上班？
   (A) Bikefarm。
   (B) Continental Railways。
   (C) Mega Maldives Airlines。
   (D) Royal Ocean Carnival。

   信件中提到 cruise vacation，與郵輪比較有相關，故含有 ocean 字樣的 Royal Ocean Carnival 比較可能是 Michael 服務的公司，得知(D)為正解。

3. 下列哪一資訊未於信中提及？
   (A) 公司將會接受錯誤票價。
   (B) 被接受之票價低於原價。
   (C) 錯誤的目的地是由某些系統錯誤而導致。
   (D) 有個非預期中的技術性問題導致錯誤的付款被執行。

由信中的 we will honor the booking which you made. 可得知，公司以消費者在訂購時所得到的票價為主，若為錯誤票價，公司也會接受；信中的 resulted in you making a payment which was much less than the original fare offered. 可知被接受之票價低於原價；由信中的 there was a system glitch where the wrong exchange rate was used in the calculation 得知非預期中的技術問題導致了匯率換算錯誤，並非搞錯目的地，故選(C)。

4. 根據此郵件，王小姐如何取得她的票券？
   (A) 她會在當地的旅行社取得票券。
   (B) 她的票券以掛號信方式寄出。
   (C) 她的票券將會附在通知信件中。
   (D) 她會在她的電子郵件附件中取得票券。

   郵件中提到 Please be informed that we have sent the electronic tickets and the itinerary receipt to you. 得知廠商將會寄出電子票券，故(D)為正解。

5. 「glitch」這個字指的是什麼？
   (A) 小問題。
   (B) 價格下降。
   (C) 增加銷售量的舉動。
   (D) 附上最新資訊的更新。

   由信中的 Based on our findings, there was a system glitch where the wrong exchange rate was used in the calculation which resulted in you making a payment much less than the original fare offered. 得知，是因為系統故障而導致價格誤植，因此可推論(A)為正解。

Unit 9

1. A   2. D   3. D   4. $8,050.   5. C

本篇為訂房確認信件。其中含有此次預約的訊息，以及各種注意事項。

1. 此信目的為何？
  (A) **確認預約。**
  (B) 提醒客人付款。
  (C) 促銷套裝旅行。
  (D) 解釋預約步驟。

  　　由信中的 Thank you for choosing to stay with us at the Premier Hotel. We are pleased to confirm your reservation 得知，此信目的為確認訂房紀錄，故(A)為正解。

2. 陳先生可能在這間飯店裡的哪一部門工作？
  (A) 客服部。
  (B) 房務部。
  (C) 人力資源部。
  (D) **訂位及櫃檯。**

  　　由於此信為訂房確認信，可知陳先生應在預約訂位相關部門工作，故(D)為正解。

3. 根據所提供之資訊，Premier Hotel 可能不會提供哪一服務？
  (A) 水療和健身。
  (B) 交通運輸。
  (C) 餐食飲料。
  (D) **民俗表演。**

  　　信中提及 spa treatments 可知飯店有提供水療服務；airport transfers，表示飯店有提供機場接送的服務；而 dining，可以得知飯店有提供餐飲服務。全信並未提及民俗表演相關資訊，故應選(D)。

4. 王小姐住宿於 Premier Hotel 兩夜應花費多少錢？

  　　由信件中表格可得知，住宿一晚要價 $3,500，兩晚則是 $7,000。且文中提到 Additional 15% rates are subjected to applicable local taxes.，得知以上價格並不含稅，因此 $7,000 須再加上 15% 才是最後總價，故 $7,000 + ($7,000 × 0.15) = $8,050。

5. 根據此信件，下列資訊何者錯誤？
  (A) 王小姐可以享受免費提早入住。
  (B) 王小姐將為她的兩晚住宿付超過 7,000 元。
  (C) **王小姐可以在她入住當天取消預訂。**
  (D) 王小姐可以透過網路表單連絡飯店。

  　　信中寫道，If you require an early check-in, please make your request as soon as possible.，可知如果需要提早入住的話，必須儘早與飯店連絡，因此王小姐可提早入住；承上題，王小姐需要付 8,050 元，超過 7,000 元；由信中的 Or by clicking <u>Contact Concierge</u> here, you will be taken to our pre-arrival checklist from where we will assist you with advance reservation 得知，點擊信件中連結「連絡服務臺人員 (Contact Concierge)」後即可連絡飯店。由信中的 If you find it necessary to cancel the reservation, the Premier Hotel requires notification by 16:00 the day before your arrival 得知，須在入住前一日的下午 4 點前通知飯店才能取消，故選(C)。

Unit 10

1. A　　2. B　　3. Plan G.

本篇為手機資費方案。 閱讀時應注意方案的內容與價錢。

1. 下列哪項產品最符合以上產品特徵？
   (A) 手機資費方案。
   (B) 卡拉 OK 器材。
   (C) 串流音樂應用程式。
   (D) 有線電視方案。

   由圖表中的 × days of unlimited data service (資料傳輸) 和 free voice call (免費語音) 等字樣，可判斷上圖為手機資費方案，故(A)為正解。

2. 以下哪一方案符合上述此產品描述？
   (A) 方案 B。
   (B) 方案 F。
   (C) 方案 G。
   (D) 方案 H。

   由 Only NT$50 per day!、 free NT$100 voice call 可知為方案 F，故選(B)。

3. Jade 下個月將會到臺灣探親。她會在那裡停留 15 天 ， 而且整段旅程都需要用到網路。她預估將會花約新臺幣 250 元的通話費。最為經濟實惠的組合方案為何？

   方案 C 加上方案 F 可以達到 Jade 的需求，但是會花費新臺幣 900 元；而方案 G 僅花費新臺幣 800 元就能達到 Jade 的需求，因此是較為經濟實惠的方案。

Living & Lifestyle

Unit 1

1. C　　2. A　　3. D　　4. A
5. NT$90 a month.

本篇為兩則訊息。 第一則是消費者對手機雲端備份容量不足的抱怨信 ； 第二則是廠商對於此客訴的回應。

1. 為何 Dianna Johns 要寫這則訊息？
   (A) 她抱怨她的新智慧型手機功能。
   (B) 她對於不到位的客戶服務感到生氣。
   (C) 她希望能有更大的免費線上備份空間。
   (D) 她在要求退回她的新智慧型手機。

   從第一則訊息的倒數第三句處 My available Cloud space is already running low after only one week of taking photos and videos 可知她的雲端備份空間根本不夠，故選(C)。

2. 下列關於 Leading Phone 對 Dianna Johns 的回應何者為真？
   (A) 該公司提供替代方案給她。
   (B) 該公司答應延長保固。
   (C) 該公司將這個錯誤怪罪到她的無知上。
   (D) 該公司承認自己服務不足。

   由 we suggest you regularly download all the files from your Cloud to any of your storage devices and then delete all of them 可知該公司提供一些建議給她參考，故選(A)。

3. 下列何字與畫底線的「notifications」一字在字義上最接近？
   (A) 專門的活動。
   (B) 檔案。
   (C) 替代方案。
   (D) 警報。

   從第一則訊息一開頭的 Recently, I've been bombarded with this annoying alert， 以及第二則訊息第二句 We are sorry for

9

bothering you with our notifications 可知，notifications 與 alert 有著對應的關係，故選(D)。

4. Dianna Johns 說「告訴我，只有 5GB 的儲存空間我要怎麼活？」這話是什麼意思？

(A) **她試著要跟該公司討價還價來獲得額外的儲存空間。**

(B) 她計畫購買他牌的新智慧型手機。

(C) 她正尋找用 5GB 雲端空間就活下來的人。

(D) 她已經說服自己只用 5GB 的雲端空間。

廠商提供的免費 5GB 雲端空間一下子就不敷使用，她非常不滿意，憤而連絡廠商，希望能獲得額外的儲存空間，故選(A)。

5. 假如 Dianna Johns 想要跟家人共享她的雲端儲存空間，她至少要花多少錢？

根據 Leading Phone 公司的回應，NT$60 a month for 100GB, NT$90 for 300GB, and NT$150 for 1TB. A new Cloud storage family sharing plan will also be available if you decide on the latter two plans。因此若要能與家人分享雲端空間，每月至少要花 90 元，故答案為 NT$90 a month。

Unit 2

1. C　　2. D　　3. B　　4. A　　5. 略。

本篇為推廣辦公室內也可以節能減碳的海報，一共列出十項辦公室綠化的小撇步。

1. 人們最有可能會在哪裡看到這張海報？

(A) 校園中。

(B) 咖啡廳裡。

(C) 辦公室裡。

(D) 圖書館裡。

由小標 Bring Greenery to Work、敘述 make your office green、green initiatives by your company 等提示可得知，場景應為辦公室，故選(C)。

2. 這幅海報的最佳標題為何？

(A) 前十種適合學生做的環保活動

(B) 讓我們一起在桌上種植栽！

(C) 綠色革命強烈建議的十件事

(D) 十種職場上簡單的節能方式

本圖文皆為辦公室場所的描述，加上該海報旨在提倡節能減碳，故選(D)。

3. 文中的「carpool」是什麼意思？

(A) 鼓勵購買二手車。

(B) 和其他人共乘同一輛車。

(C) 藉由買電動車以降低空氣汙染。

(D) 藉由騎腳踏車上班以節約能源。

由 Bike/Carpool to Work 中的圖片可以推論，Carpool 是一群人共乘一輛車，是一種省錢又環保的方法，故選(B)。

4. 下列哪一項描述在海報中沒有被提及？

(A) 一次性容器增加了清潔人員的工作量。

(B) 鼓勵用可重複使用的水瓶或馬克杯喝水。

(C) 每個小改變都會對環境有所影響。

(D) 無紙的環境是我們企圖達成的目標之一。

Avoid Disposable Cups 寫到，停止使用一次性容器，並攜帶自己的水瓶或馬克杯來喝水；Join Green Initiatives 與 Lend

Your Support 則寫到 Every bit counts 和 Every voice matters，意即我們做的任何改變都會對環境有所影響；最後在海報中的 Say No to Printing 中可以發現，在這個數位時代，能夠全面使用電子郵件以及雲端是人們努力的方向。僅(A)沒被提到，故選(A)。

5. 身為學生，你可以做什麼來幫助教室更加綠意盎然？
  略。

Unit 3

1. ⊠　2. A　3. D　4. B　5. B

本篇為洗滌圖示說明。圖一為五種最基本的洗滌標示。圖二為實際出現在衣物上的洗滌標示名牌。圖三則是說明常出現在洗滌標示上的其他標記。

1. 請畫出「請勿滾筒烘乾」的圖示。
  圖二中說明滾筒烘乾的圖形為正方形中含有一個圓形，圖三的交叉圖形意為禁止的意思，故此題的圖示應該畫成 ⊠。

2. 這篇文章主要的目的為何？
  (A) **教讀者如何閱讀洗滌標籤。**
  (B) 介紹洗滌標籤的歷史。
  (C) 比較兩種不同的洗滌標籤。
  (D) 推廣一款新式的洗滌標籤系統。
  　本文從圖一開始介紹五種基本洗滌標籤的圖示，接著在圖二介紹實際上看到的標籤樣貌，又在圖三說明更多常用於洗滌標籤上的標記，主要在教讀者如何閱讀洗滌標籤，故選(A)。

3. 下列何者並未在文章中提及？
  (A) 洗滌標籤的功能。
  (B) 看懂洗滌標籤的小技巧。
  (C) 為何要看懂洗滌標籤上的圖示的原因。
  (D) **將洗滌標籤標在衣服上的規定。**
  　文章一開始提到 Symbols on a care label tag provide helpful information about the garment we are going to buy，即是在說明洗滌標籤的功能為提供關於我們即將要買的衣服的洗滌資訊；而三張圖表皆是在教讀者看懂洗滌標籤的技巧。在文末寫到 Therefore, pay careful attention to the care label tags and follow the directions in order to look after your clothes properly，則強調看懂洗滌標籤可以更妥善地保養自己的衣服。但文中並未明確指出如果要把洗滌標籤標在衣服上需要哪些條件，故選(D)。

4. 畫底線的 pre-shrunk 一字是什麼意思？

(A) 由某些水洗就會縮水的衣料所組成。

(B) 不會因為水洗而再縮得更小。

(C) 藉由明確列出指示而使其更容易辨認。

(D) 使其保持完美無缺來讓衣服保存得更好。

文中 "100% combed ring spun cotton pre-shrunk" tells the consumers that the garment is made of cotton and that the clothing has been made smaller by washing before being sold 表示 pre-shrunk 意指在出售之前已經事先水洗過讓尺寸變小，如此一來售出後大小就不會再變，故選(B)。

5. 下列哪一描述符合以下圖中所列的洗滌標籤？

(A) 僅能用手洗且不能漂白、乾洗或整燙。

(B) 使用弱速、中溫的滾筒烘乾。

(C) 使用水溫最高攝氏 40 度的免燙衣物洗程。

(D) 低溫整燙與含氧漂白劑限定。

此標籤是 100% 丙烯酸纖維織物；由左至右依序為機洗水溫限定 40 度以下、不可漂白、可使用滾筒中溫烘乾但需低速運轉、可乾洗、以及可低溫整燙。故選(B)。

Unit 4

1. D　　2. C　　3. A

4. The Bowman Show at East Front Jimmy watched ended at 1:50 p.m., and he took some time to have a rest. He wouldn't know the exact time of "History Tours" until he got there. There is not enough information about "The Castle Dungeon," and Jimmy just missed the last chance to see "Flight of the Eagles" because it had started at 2:00 p.m. So, "The Mighty Trebuchet" is the only available show for Jimmy to watch.

本篇為遊樂園表演節目表以及遊樂園地圖。第一張海報列出展演的名稱、地點與時間。第二張圖則詳細標出遊樂園各個遊樂設施的所在位置。

1. 這張海報給了什麼資訊？

(A) 每場表演的詳細資訊。

(B) 這些長期表演的價格。

(C) 人們可以買到票的地方。

(D) 不同表演的時刻表與地點。

由第一張圖內的名稱、地點與時間可知，這是不同場次表演的時刻表與地點，故選(D)。

2. 下列敘述何者正確？

(A) Jimmy 可以在 Great Hall Entrance 買到所有表演的票。

(B) Jimmy 可以在 The Courtyard Shop 隨時看到「Flight of the Eagles」。

(C) Jimmy 將在 Great Hall Entrance 知道他何時可以看到 History Tours。

(D) 「The Castle Dungeon」 這個表演將在 Riverside Arena 演出。

圖片中並未提及可以在哪裡買票；而 Flight of the Eagles 的表演場地為 Birds of Prey Arena，並非 The Courtyard Shop；最後 The Castle Dungeon 的地點在 The Courtyard Shop。根據 History Tours 的描述 Times at location ，可以得知要到了 Great Hall Entrance 才會知道時間，故選(C)。

3. 根據 Jimmy 的行程，哪一個表演是 Jimmy 接下來一定可以看到的？

(A) **The Mighty Trebuchet**。

(B) Flight of the Eagles。

(C) The Castle Dungeon。

(D) None of the above。

　　現在時間已經是下午 2 點 20 分。根據海報上的時間表，只有 The Mighty Trebuchet 在下午 4 點還有場次，故選 (A)。

4. 以下是三民遊樂園的地圖。請畫出 Jimmy 如何從目前所在之處到達他想看的下一場節目。此外，根據所給資訊，解釋第三題答案的理由。

(1) 畫圖：略。(2) 現在是下午 2 點 20 分，Flight of the Eagles 的最後一場時間為下午 2 點，Jimmy 已經錯過了；The Castle Dungeon 的資訊不完整，而只有下午 4 點開演的 The Mighty Trebuchet 對 Jimmy 而言一定可以看到，故選 (C)。

Unit 5

1. D　　2. Parents.　　3. A　　4. C

本篇為玩具賣場的廣告，上面告知讀者玩具店的地點、交通方式、營業時間、販賣哪些類別的商品以及提供哪些服務。

1. 看 ToysFunKidsCome (TFKC) 的廣告。何者在廣告中未被提及？

(A) 店家地址。

(B) 店家營業時間。

(C) 小孩可以在戶外玩的車子。

(D) **顧客對於店家的評論。**

　　店名下面有提供地址；由 Open 'til Late 那欄的訊息可得知營業時間；由 Outdoor play, sports, and ride on vehicles 則可得知，店家也有賣戶外的玩具車。圖片中並沒有顯示顧客對於該店家的評論，故選 (D)。

2. 根據提供的資訊，家中成員裡，誰可能是這家店的主要常客？

　　這家販售的商品為玩具、遊戲、婦嬰用品、(三輪) 腳踏車、戶外用品，因此最合適的答案為家長 (parents)。

3. 大家都說 TFKC 以他們的貼心服務聞名。根據廣告，下列哪一服務他們並未提供？

(A) **幫忙家長照顧小孩。**

(B) 提供顧客免費停車場。

(C) 大部分晚上都有營業。

(D) 提供線上購物平臺。

　　海報中提到店家提供 free on-site parking；店家週一到週六都營業到晚上十點；且由文中的 Click & Collect @toysfuns.co.uk 可以得知，店家有提供購物網站。海報中並未提到有幫忙家長照顧孩童的服務，故選 (A)。

4. 住在 Brent Cross 一帶的 Peng 太太想要買兒童三輪車給她的姪子當生日禮物。她被告知 TFKC 所有的玩具正在特賣。下列何者不會是她的選項？

(A) 搭 70 與 210 號公車到實體商店。

(B) 致電 0208-666-1717 洽詢更深入的資訊。

(C) **星期天晚上帶她的姪子去商店。**

(D) 從購物中心搭 Circle Line。

海報中提到從 Brent Cross 商場到玩具店的交通方式，其中一個就是搭 70 和 210 號公車；而消費者若有任何想知道的訊息，都可以撥打 0208-666-1717 給他們的顧問；同時海報中也有提到可以從 Brent Cross 購物中心搭地鐵 Circle Line 到他們的實體商店。海報中有提到 TFKC 的營業時間，不過星期天最晚只營業到下午 5 點，故選(C)。

Unit 6

1. B   2. C   3. B   4. June 10th.

本篇為圖書館使用條款同意書，內容在告知讀者必須先簽署這份條約才能開始在圖書館借閱書籍，以及一些借書的相關規則。

1. 這一份資訊的來源是？

(A) 書店的傳單。

(B) **圖書館的網頁。**

(C) 線上遊戲的登入頁面。

(D) 圖書館員的抱怨信。

　　由文中 You are required to sign the "Terms of Use Agreement" before you are allowed to borrow from the library，到最後須填入 User ID、Password 與 Send 鍵等介面，可觀察出這個資訊是來自於圖書館的網頁，故選(B)。

2. 誰可能會需要簽署這份同意書？

(A) 所有 Sanmin 大學的師生。

(B) 建造 Sanmin 大學的贊助者。

(C) **任何首次想要來圖書館借書的人。**

(D) 任何需要借閱已被預約的書的人。

　　從 You are required to sign the "Terms of User Agreement" before you are allowed to borrow from the library，可知對象為第一次來圖書館借書的人，故選(C)。

3. Linda 終於在 6 月 4 日成功在圖書館借到了她最愛的連載小說最新一集。不過，她同時被告知有人也預訂了同一本書，那麼她必須在何時歸還這本書？

(A) 6 月 10 日。

(B) **6 月 17 日。**

(C) 6 月 24 日。

(D) 7 月 1 日。

　　根據條款中的 The library will enforce a recall policy if the item you intend to borrow has also been reserved by others—the borrowing period for the item will be shortened to 14 days。因此，她只能借閱

14 天，最晚得在 6 月 17 日前完成歸還動作，故選(B)。

4. 為了做報告，Willy 借了片紀錄片 DVD 半個月。然而這片 DVD 在今日 (6 月 4 日) 被一位教授預約。Willy 得在哪天前歸還 DVD？

Willy 已借了超過 14 天，根據條款 2: please return the item within 7 days after you have received the notification. 可知，當一樣東西借了超過 14 天後突然有人預訂，那就必須在接到通知後的 7 天內歸還。因此他應該在 6 月 10 日前歸還，故答案為 June 10th。

Unit 7

1. C　2. C　3. A　4. $24.5.

本圖為一個公告，告知遊客大教堂因為外借場地而短暫關閉，開放時間與門票費用也會因此有所調整。

1. 根據這公告，哪一群人最不會被這個活動影響？
   (A) 想看大教堂內部的遊客。
   (B) 大教堂內的紀念品商店店員。
   (C) 來參加大教堂婚禮的客人。
   (D) 每週打掃大教堂的管理人員。

   這則公告是針對教堂外借他人舉辦婚禮一事而對教堂開放時間與門票做出調整，影響層面當然會涉及前來參觀的遊客，也會影響教堂內商店店員及清潔人員的工作時間。但因參加婚禮的人原本並不會來到教堂，不屬於受到影響的人，因此選(C)。

2. 根據公告，下列敘述何者正確？
   (A) 有一對佳偶已於教堂結婚了。
   (B) 中午將會舉行一場婚宴。
   (C) 自下午 1 點 30 分起教堂部分地區會關閉。
   (D) 教堂僅開放早上供遊客參觀。

   由公告上的 and part of the cathedral will be temporarily closed to visitors from 1:30 p.m. 可知，故選(C)。

3. 下列何者與畫底線的「accordingly」一字在字義上最相近？
   (A) 結果。
   (B) 故意。
   (C) 偶然地。
   (D) 某種程度上。

   according 的前一句提到教堂的部分區域會關閉，本句則是在說入場費用會有所調整，由此可知這兩句話之間是因果關係，故選(A)。

4. 11 歲的 Elizabeth 對建築很有興趣。她邀請父母在 9 月 15 日這天一同前往教堂。他們家有五個人。除了爸媽外，還有一名超過 65 歲的爺爺與一位正在學步走的弟弟。一行人在下午 1 點抵達現場。他們需要花多少錢入場？

根據當天調整後的入場費用，他們可以購買家庭票再加一張敬老票最便宜，即 $18 + $6.5 = $24.5。

Unit 8

1. B   2. C   3. D   4. Preschoolers.   5. C

本篇為介紹 Sanmin 動物園在暑假期間所舉辦的活動公告。

1. 下列哪一款海報最能描述以上資訊？
   (A) 在動物園野生露營。
   (B) 加入 Sanmin 動物園的野性平日。
   (C) 在樹蔭裡野生探險。
   (D) 在浪花島與熊一起消暑。

   告示牌上提到活動時間為 7 月 2 日到 8 月 31 日的平日，能詳細列出每週一到五有哪些活動的海報是最好的選擇，故選 (B)。

2. 為何 Sanmin 動物園要辦一系列的暑期活動？
   (A) 為了增加園方夏季的營收。
   (B) 為了在短時間內提升園方的知名度。
   (C) 為了替野生動物保育與氣候關注發聲。
   (D) 為了替 Sanmin 動物園裡瀕危動物募款。

   由告示最後一段可知，園方所設計的活動都是用來提高遊客對於野生動物保育以及氣候議題的關注，故選(C)。

根據上方圖片的資訊，觀察下方圖片並回答下列兩個問題。

3. 他們正在參加什麼活動？
   (A) 動物園畫畫日。
   (B) 卡通玩偶見面會。
   (C) 做瑜珈放鬆。
   (D) 在野生動物保健中心為動物玩偶做健檢。

   由圖片中可看到參加的人帶著自己的玩偶去看醫生，在告示牌中有提到 Preschoolers are encouraged to bring their favorite animal toy dolls for a check-up by the vet at Sanmin Zoo every Wednesday。表示他們在進行玩偶健檢活動，故選(D)。

4. 遊客中的哪個族群最可能參加這個活動？
  承第三題的解析可知，這項活動主要是設計給學齡前兒童參加的，故答案為 preschoolers。

5. 閱讀以下資訊，關於這項服務，下列何者為真？
  (A) 小孩可以在這個活動跟他們最喜歡的角色打招呼。
  (B) 人們可以在電影表定時間前 15 分鐘購買快速通關票券。
  (C) 喜愛看電影的人也許會對這個活動非常有興趣。
  (D) 這個活動在 Special Events Center 入口處舉行。
  文中並沒有說這個活動會不會有真實的電影角色出現與觀眾相見歡；快速通關票券可在電影開演前 24 小時購買。除此之外，這個活動是在 Special Events Center 內部舉行的，而非入口。這則資訊是在介紹 Sanmin 動物園於每週二都歡迎社區民眾與遊客一同欣賞經典電影，故選(C)。

Unit 9

1. C 2. D 3. B 4. $600；12/31/2023.

本篇為介紹罰單的明細以及一些注意事項，包含違規事項、地點以及員警編號等等。

1. 根據以上資訊，我們可以得知這表格是什麼？
  (A) 停車許可證。
  (B) 停車場收據。
  (C) 交通罰單。
  (D) 駕照。
  由幾個關鍵字：infringement (違反)、offence (罪行)、penalty (處罰)、vehicle details (車輛細節) 等資訊可知，這是一張交通違規通知單，即俗稱的罰單，故選(C)。

2. 此人違反了什麼規則？
  (A) 酒駕。
  (B) 超速。
  (C) 闖紅燈。
  (D) 違規停車。
  由被指控的罪行 (Alleged Offence) 可以得知，這輛車是在不可停車的地方停車，因此選(D)。

3. 下列哪個敘述在本文中沒有被提到？
  (A) 一輛 Toyota 汽車違反 Papaya City 中的 R101 法規。
  (B) 車主可以在位於 Gettysburg Street 的 City Hall 繳罰金。
  (C) 此次違規發生在十一月某個上午的 Gettysburg Street。
  (D) 警察編號 PPA12 的這位員警負責這項違規。
  文中並未提到位在 Gettysburg Street 上的 City Hall 可以繳罰金，故選(B)。

4. 這張罰單的罰金是多少？繳交期限為何？
  由 Penalty 與 Due Date 兩個資訊可知，罰金為 600 元；繳費期限為 2023 年 12 月 31 日。

Unit 10

1. The government at the time had limited budget.
2. A　　3. C　　4. B　　5. B

本篇在介紹位於蘇格蘭泰河上鄧凱爾德橋的牌匾,並說明當初建造這座橋的歷史。

1. 為何建立鄧凱爾德橋需要用公用事業民營化這個模式?

   文章中提到 However, due to a limited budget, the government at the time worked on a private-public partnership scheme,可知當初在建造橋樑的時候預算是有限的。

2. 橋墩上的牌匾功能為何?

   (A) 它被用來提醒人們某個重要的人物或事件。

   (B) 它指引觀光客附近的景點方向。

   (C) 它訴說著將會留名青史的趣聞。

   (D) 它寫著埋葬名人的地址。

   這個牌匾是為了紀念鄧凱爾德橋建造滿兩百週年 (bicentenary),因此牌匾上的文字是用來提醒人們某些重要的人事物,故選(A)。

3. 下列關於牌匾的敘述何者為真?

   (A) 它由 Thomas Telford 的後代製作。

   (B) 它在鄧凱爾德橋建好後隨即設立。

   (C) 它記載著過橋費何時停止徵收。

   (D) 它由 Thomas Telford 於 1766 年設計。

   圖中只有寫揭幕 (unveil) 的人為 John 11th Duke of Atholl,而非 Thomas Telford 的後代;該牌匾揭幕時間為 2009 年,表示這個牌匾並非在鄧凱爾德橋建好後就立即掛置;Thomas Telford 是設計了這座橋,但並未提及是否在 1766 年設計。由牌匾上 Built . . . as a major element in the improvement of highland roads by replacing two ferries and paid for by tolls until taken over by the roads authority in 1879 可知,它記錄何時停止徵收過橋費。故選(C)。

4. 下列哪一原因不能解釋為何當時政府急切地想在鄧凱爾德這區的泰河上蓋橋?

   (A) 泰河上的渡輪在高水位時很危險。

   (B) 提高通往高地的交通運量很迫切。

   (C) 泰河的交通運量一直都很大。

   (D) 意外事故與天災已奪取許多人的生命。

   根據文章前三句話可知政府蓋橋的原因。而此橋蓋好才反而使通往高地的交通狀況大增 (making it both functional—carrying the bulk of the traffic into the Highlands),故選(B)。

5. 下列哪一片語與畫底線的片語「cough up」字義最為相近?

   (A) 負責任。

   (B) 花錢。

   (C) 放棄。

   (D) 停留在。

   根據描述 As the cost spiraled out of control, to far more than the government could pay, the Duke had no choice but to cough up the rest of the sum, hence making it necessary for placing tolls on the bridge 可知,當時建橋費用失控且不停攀升,政府無力負擔。導致公爵最後只好自掏腰包,還得設置過橋費,由此推敲出 cough up for the rest 是勉強掏錢付剩下的費用,故選(B)。

Food & Drink

Unit 1

本篇為咖啡種類圖。閱讀時應注意各種咖啡的異同，以及各種咖啡的原料。

1. 上述這些咖啡飲品，最主要的不同處為何？

   圖表標示出各種咖啡品項的內容物，因此可以得知主要是以「成分」和「比例」區別出不同的咖啡種類。

2. 根據以上的咖啡飲品表，一位平常需要兩倍濃縮咖啡的顧客可能會點何種飲品來開啟新的一天？

   (A) 愛爾蘭咖啡。

   (B) 雙份濃縮咖啡。

   (C) 拿鐵咖啡。

   (D) 美式咖啡。

   Doppio 是義大利文「兩倍」的意思，包含了兩倍濃縮咖啡，符合該顧客需求，故選(B)。

3. 乳糖為一種自然的糖分，通常會在乳製品中發現。以下何種咖啡飲品適合無法分解乳糖的人？

   (A) 拿鐵瑪琪朵。

   (B) 焦糖瑪琪朵。

   (C) 卡布奇諾。

   (D) 美式咖啡。

   由圖表可知，Latte Macchiato、Caramel Macchiato 和 Cappuccino 皆具有牛奶成分，Americano 則無，因此 Americano 適合無法分解乳糖的人，故選(D)。

4. 用自己的話解釋此菜單。

   本題可自由填寫，建議可以由原料、組合來分析各種咖啡飲品。

Unit 2

本篇為食譜。閱讀時請注意各個步驟，以及各原料的分量及備料、烘焙方法。

1. 此文章目的為何？

   (A) 列出能被預訂和供應的餐點。

   (B) 解釋如何經營一家餐廳。

   (C) 標示大部分包裝食物所需的成分。

   (D) 教導如何用多種食材做出食物。

   由以上提到的步驟 1 到步驟 4，可知此篇文章是講述程序的說明文，且內容提及食材和烹飪方法，因此正解為(D)。

2. 上述文章是什麼？

   文章中依序寫下食材和烹飪料理的方式，可以得知此篇是食譜。

3. 這段文字是由一位主廚所寫的。以下哪個餐廳可能是這位主廚服務的餐廳？

   (A) 泰式海鮮攤販。

   (B) 義大利披薩屋。

   (C) 日本壽司吧。

   (D) 中華料理餐廳。

   由步驟 3 第 1 句逗號後方 knock out the air and roll it into a base the same size as a large frying pan 可推測，會將麵團中的空氣擠壓出來，並滾成與大平底鍋同一尺寸的食物，成品應為披薩，故選(B)。

4. 第二段的「season」一字文意為何？

   (A) 增添風味。

   (B) 切成小塊。

   (C) 壓成塊狀。

   (D) 放置一季。

   由前句 making sure the garlic doesn't brown, and then add the tomato sauce. Season well and bubble simmer for 8–10 minutes until you have a rich sauce—add a pinch of sugar if it tastes a little too tart. 可知是在講述製作醬料的步驟，故選(A)。

5. 請在步驟 1 前寫一句介紹句。

若要在步驟 1 前加上一句介紹句，應該要是介紹本文主旨的標題句，可在此句指出本食譜的目標及特色。This recipe ensures a crispy-bottomed pizza without ever turning on the oven. 明確講述了這個披薩便於製作的特色。

Unit 3

1. B　2. Purple.　3. B
4. I disagree that people eat the food often. Although the food contains no cholesterol at all, it still has high proportions of saturated fat, and, therefore, may cause our body to produce cholesterol. In other words, even though we do not have direct intake of cholesterol, high amount of saturated fat is still associated with increased risk of coronary heart disease.

本篇為食品標籤。上面標示了某食品各營養素的含量，以及建議每日攝取量的百分比。閱讀時除注意以上訊息外，需特別注意此營養標籤所標示的分量為何。

1. 以下敘述中，哪一項關於上述食物的描述是正確的？

(A) 此食物一包含 547 卡路里。

(B) 此食物含有相當多的鹽分與脂肪。

(C) 此食物一包未達到每日脂肪所需。

(D) 此食物包含了高比例的蛋白質來幫助肌肉成長。

由 2 servings per container、Serving size 100g、Amount per serving Calories 547 得知，每 100 公克食物含 547 卡路里，且一個包裝有兩份，因此一包應含有 1,094 卡路里；由 Total Fat (脂肪)：57% 可得知，該食物一份含 57% 的每日建議油脂攝取量，本包裝含有兩份，即超過建議攝取量；這項食物一份的蛋白質 (Protein) 只有 6.56 公克，脂肪卻有 37.47 公克，碳水化合物則是有 49.74 公克，與其他營養素相比，蛋白質比例偏低。由 Total Fat：57% 及 Sodium (鈉)：21% 得知油和鹽分別為建議每日攝取量的 57% 和 21%，含有相當多的油與鹽分，故 (B) 正確。

2. 下圖為 4 個重要營養素 (脂肪、膽固醇、鈉與碳水化合物) 的一天建議攝取量圓餅圖。根據食品標籤，請問哪個顏色代表碳水化合物？

由此圖所示，未標出顏色的有碳水化合物跟脂肪，搭配上食物標籤資訊可以得知，一天建議碳水化合物攝取量約為 49.74 ÷ 16% ≒ 311 (g)，而脂肪為 37.47 ÷ 57% ≒ 66 (g)，可知碳水化合物應是占最大比例的紫色。

3. 題目中的食物標籤最有可能指的是下列哪一食品？

(A) 水果沙拉。

(B) 洋芋片。

(C) 西瓜汁。

(D) 番茄海鮮湯。

　　由食物標籤資訊得知，此食物最大比例營養素為脂肪，四種食物相較之下，洋芋片的油脂含量最高，因此正解為(B)。

4. 根據以下敘述，你是否同意「人們常吃這種食物會有好處」這件事？

　　由題目所提供的營養資訊可知，此食物雖然膽固醇含量為0，但脂肪總量超過50%，且當中的不飽和脂肪更是超過50%，這會使我們的身體製造更多膽固醇，因而拉高冠狀動脈心臟疾病的風險，所以人們應該要少吃一點這類食品。

Unit 4

1. A　　2. Tri-State Area.　　3. D

4. I determined the nutrition facts of this dish by looking into the different nutrition weights. A is lacking fat; B is lacking salt; C is lacking protein. That is why I chose D.

本篇為食物介紹的螢幕截圖。除標題外，應觀察說明文字來判斷網頁的功能。

1. 以下何圖會在此螢幕截圖中出現？

(A) 糖醋排骨。

(B) 牛排。

(C) 豬肉蔬菜湯。

(D) 漢堡。

　　由 Stir-fry bite-sized pork with a sweet and sour sauce made of sugar, ketchup, white vinegar, and soy sauce. 可知此敘述指的是酸甜風味的(A)糖醋排骨。

2. 請問此顧客是在哪一地區嘗試尋找餐廳？

　　從此螢幕截圖最上面的部分得知此顧客在三川地區尋找餐廳。

3. 以下哪一食品標示最符合此道菜？

　　仔細觀察可知(A)選項的脂肪只有1公克；(B)選項不含鹽分；(C)選項不含蛋白質，唯獨(D)選項的各項成分較符合糖醋排骨的營養比例，故選(D)。

4. 基於第三題，你是以何種原則來判斷這道菜的食品標示？

　　承上題，各項營養成分是判斷此題食品標示的主要原則。

Unit 5

1. B　2. D　3. C→B→D→A　4. 5.

本篇介紹學校外燴規定。內含注意事項及各種規定與預約時間相關內容。

1. 請問人們可能在哪裡看到此公告？
   (A) 大學學年行事曆通知。
   (B) 大學餐飲服務網站。
   (C) 當地學校午餐餐廳。
   (D) 城市旅遊資訊中心。
   　　內文主要介紹大學餐飲事項，故選(B)。

2. 此公告包含以下何種服務項目？
   (A) 線上取消。
   (B) 全年無休的服務。
   (C) 派對裝飾服務。
   (D) 取貨和地區性外送。
   　　公告中雖有 Cancellations，但由 To cancel catered events, campus delivery, and takeout orders, contact Campus Scheduling at (208) 496–3120. 可知，取消須以電話通知，而非網路；由 University Catering does not take orders for catered events, deliveries, or takeout orders on Sundays or Monday nights after 5:00 p.m. 可得知，週日全天和週一下午5點後沒有餐飲服務，並非全年無休；此公告無任何「派對 (party)」和「裝飾 (decoration)」相關字彙。由 Types of Catering Service University Catering Provides 子項目中的 Delivery services to campus locations、Off-campus delivery on an exception basis to University approved off-campus events 以及 Takeout orders for the campus and community 可知，大學餐廳包含區域性外送和外帶服務，故選(D)。

3. 根據以上公告，請排列以下步驟之先後順序。
   (A) 免費取消。
   (B) 菜單與服務細節的最終確認。
   (C) 活動經營處的餐會許可。
   (D) 活動與外送的事先付費。
   　　(A)由 there is no charge for cancellations made at least three business days prior to a scheduled event. 可知免費取消須於活動當日前三個工作天完成；(B)由 Menus and service details should be finalized seven days prior to the scheduled event. 可知，菜單和服務細節的確認須於活動當日前七個工作天完成；(C)由 Once the event is approved by Campus Scheduling, contact University Catering to place a catered event order as far in advance as possible. 可知一旦活動日期被同意，就要儘早確認訂單；(D)由 University Catering requires that each event and delivery order be prepaid six days before the scheduled event. 可知預付款項須於活動當日前六個工作天完成。綜合以上資訊得知此四步驟順序為：(C) → (B) → (D) → (A)。

4. 根據公告，每星期有幾晚可以接受訂單？
   由 University Catering does not take orders for catered events, deliveries, or takeout orders on Sundays or Monday nights after 5:00 p.m. 得知，週一跟週日不接受訂單，故可以知道答案應是去掉此兩天的 5 天。

Unit 6

1. Lasagne.　2. C　3. C　4. 略

本篇為介紹料理的各種組成要素的傳單。注意每個解釋所指的地方以及讓此食物與眾不同的關鍵字。

1. 根據以上傳單所提供的線索，這是何種義大利麵？

由圖片中的 15-layer Lasagne 可知是千層麵 (Lasagne)。

2. 以下何者不包括在此義大利麵料理中？
   (A) 香腸。
   (B) 牛肉肉醬。
   (C) 巧達起司。
   (D) 微型裝飾。

   由圖片中的 Grandma's handmade seasoned sausage 可知其中含有香腸 (sausage)；由圖片中的 Grandma's special sauce mixed with fresh tomatoes and beef meat 可知，此麵食包含牛肉肉醬；由 Miniature Italian flag on the top of the 15-layer Lasagne 可知，此麵食上方有著國旗小裝飾。在圖片中無提及任何起司字樣，故(C)選項並無包含在此菜餚中。

3. 以下敘述何者最接近傳單中的「Made-from-Scratch」？
   (A) 提供在工廠就預先準備好的食物。
   (B) 只吃質地柔軟的食物。
   (C) 以原型食材而非半加工食材來做菜。
   (D) 提供增加風味而非營養的人工香料所製成的餐點。

   由傳單上的 Made-from-Scratch Home Made Cooking 可知 Made-from-Scratch 是用來描述 Homemade Cooking，意即所有餐點皆是以手工製作，隱喻不使用已半完工的加工食材，而是使用新鮮食材製成，故選(C)。

4. 根據大廚的說法，是什麼讓這道義大利麵料理如此「不可思議」？

由報導標題即知此報導在說明此菜餚「不可思議」的原因，如：15-layer Lasagne、made-from-scratch ingredients、special sauce、three days to prepare，抓住關鍵字即可回答本題。

Unit 7

1. D   2. A   3. Red or Green Burrito.
4. 70 cents.

本篇為餐廳菜單。閱讀時請特別注意各品項的名稱、價錢與內容物。

1. 這家餐廳提供何種食物？
   (A) 燉菜。
   (B) 速食。
   (C) 乳製品。
   (D) 素食。
   由菜單上出現的 Vegetarian、Veggie、BRC (Beans, Rice, and Cheese)、Bean & Cheese 字樣可知此餐廳應是素食餐廳，故選(D)。

2. 此菜單內容用什麼來分類？
   (A) 食物項目。
   (B) 餐點價錢。
   (C) 攝入的卡路里。
   (D) 烹調方式。
   由菜單上的子標題 (Tacos、Quesadillas、Burritos、Sandwiches) 可知此菜單是以不同的菜色種類做區隔，故選(A)。

3. 以下描述為菜單上的某項料理，請問指的是哪道菜？
   從 gently wrapped in a home-made tortilla 可知它是捲餅類的商品，再加上後面對紅綠兩種醬的描述可知這道料理應該是 Red or Green Burrito。

4. 一位購買「Bean & Cheese burrito」的顧客需要額外付多少錢才能將餐點升級為包含米飯？
   由菜單得知 Bean & Cheese burrito 要價 $1.59，而此餐點若想升級為含米飯，成為 $2.29 的 BRC burrito (Beans, Rice, and Cheese)，則需要再加上兩者的差價，故答案為 70 分。

Unit 8

1. A   2. Anyone who is in need.   3. A
4. Those who exhibit disruptive or disorderly conduct.

本篇為咖啡廳提供待用咖啡的公告。類似的公告通常會貼在餐廳或咖啡廳內，介紹待用咖啡的執行方式與相關注意事項。

1. 請問何謂「suspended coffee」？
   (A) 顧客為有需要的人所購買的咖啡。
   (B) 顧客為募款製作的咖啡。
   (C) 老闆為慶祝商店周年慶為顧客免費製作的咖啡。
   (D) 為支持全球農夫公平交易的咖啡。
   由傳單中的 We'll serve the item to a patron in need. 可知此咖啡是為有需要的人所設，而購買方式則由 To purchase a suspended coffee, just tell the cashier what you would like to add to your order and pay. 可知是由顧客付費購買，故選(A)。

2. 什麼樣的人有資格收到待用咖啡？
   由傳單中的 We'll serve the item to a patron in need. 可知此咖啡是為有需要的人所設，故「有需要的人」即為正解。

3. 以下哪一口號適合此「待用咖啡活動」？
   (A) 不只是一杯咖啡。
   (B) 蒸餾出的正義就在你手上。
   (C) 值得喝第二杯的風味。
   (D) 從產地直送到你杯中。
   由第一題和第二題可得知，此活動並非僅僅只是為了喝咖啡，而是為有需要之人付出一己之力，故選(A)。

4. 怎樣的人不被歡迎參加此活動？
   由傳單中最後一段的文字 This establishment reserves the right to refuse service to any patron who exhibits disruptive or disorderly conduct. 可知任何做破壞性行為或不守規矩的人都不受歡迎。

Unit 9

> 1. Fresh fruit.
> 2. Americans are continuing to increase their consumption of fresh fruits and vegetables while decreasing their consumption of processed fruit and vegetables.
> 3. C　　4. C

本折線圖顯示美國歷年蔬果消費趨勢。觀察隨年度變化的各種不同蔬果，並針對其增減進行分析。

1. 此四種類中 (加工蔬菜、新鮮蔬菜、加工水果及新鮮水果)，哪一類的消費在這些年呈現穩定成長？

   在此四類中，processed fruit 是唯一趨勢呈現減少的種類，故此類不符合題目要素。其他三類在 2013–2016 年皆呈現成長，但過了 2016 年後，卻只有 fresh fruit 繼續成長，故 fresh fruit 為正解。

2. 根據下列分析，請解釋美國蔬果消費習慣如何變化？

   從上文可知，美國人減少加工食品的消費，且增加新鮮蔬果的消費。

3. 根據以上分析，什麼導致美國蔬果消費習慣改變？

   (A) 美國經濟轉變。

   (B) 美國農業的演進。

   (C) 美國民眾健康意識的提高。

   (D) 美國健康保險系統的轉變。

   根據上面短文所述，大部分公共健康和營養專家表示美國人在肥胖、癌症和其他健康疑慮下，選擇多攝取新鮮蔬果，因為被調理加工過的食物通常含有較高的鹽分和糖分，健康意識逐漸抬頭，故選(C)。

4. 假如美國政府想要持續鼓勵新鮮蔬果的消費，以下何種策略可能會是必要的？

   (A) 盡可能使用高效率的長距離運送方法。

   (B) 持續在製造和配送系統上減少浪費。

   (C) 鼓勵當地作物以創造實際的「當季」經濟。

(D) 發展像是即時冷凍以維持口感及營養的保存方式。

由上文可知，(A)選項中的「長距離」和(D)選項中的「即時冷凍」皆與「罐頭和冷凍蔬果持續減少」或「新鮮蔬果增加」相違背。故(C)選項為正解。

Unit 10

1. B　　2. D
3. "There is not enough investment in better farming techniques, transportation, and storage, which means lost income for small farmers and higher prices for poor consumers."
4. 略

本篇為單格漫畫。閱讀時須注意人物的對話、所做的動作、穿的衣服與道具等，用以判斷漫畫的主題。

1. 請問這張圖試著強調什麼議題？
　(A) 食物保存和安全性。
　(B) 食物浪費和飢餓。
　(C) 食物毒性和傳染性微生物。
　(D) 食物短缺和氣候變遷。
　　由圖中肥胖的人和骨瘦如柴的人所呈現的對比，及前者手中充沛的食物對照後者看著垃圾桶捱餓的無奈，可看出本圖想要探討食物浪費和飢餓的議題。

2. 此插圖傳達什麼樣的態度？
　(A) 樂觀的。
　(B) 疑惑的。
　(C) 懷疑的。
　(D) 諷刺的。
　　由肥胖的人和骨瘦如柴的人所呈現的對比，可知本圖要呈現出諷刺挖苦的態度。

3. 以下段落與上圖有關。仔細閱讀並嘗試找出下文中關於發展中國家所面對的問題之句子。
　　本段落中提到，「沒有足夠的金錢投資在更好的農耕技術、交通運輸和食物保存上，意味著小農損失了收入，而貧窮的消費者要用更高的價錢購買農產品」，點出發展中國家的問題；因為這些問題，所以食物容易腐爛，而本來就貧窮的消費者則須拿出更多收入去購買稀少的食物，造成惡性循環。

4. 閱讀此漫畫後，4 個人有不同想法，你最同意誰？為什麼？
　A：如果食物和法拉利一樣貴，人們就會將它擦亮且好好照顧它。
　B：當一個人肚子飽了，他是否有錢便沒有差別。
　C：人們想要真實的、富有風味的食物，而不是準備了數天卻只為了炫耀的食物。
　D：當世界存在著如此飢餓的人們時，上帝就只能以麵包的形式現身了。

本題可以自由發揮，選擇你最同意的一句，並利用關鍵字寫出原因。

Mass Communication

Unit 1

1. Household.　2. B　3. A　4. C　5. C

本圖為澳洲廢棄物來源報告及其掩埋回收的情況。廢棄物總共分為三大來源：工商業廢棄物、建築拆除廢棄物和家庭廢棄物。

1. 根據以上圖表，哪一類廢棄物回收的數量比被掩埋的數量還低？

   根據圖表內的數值可以得知，家庭廢棄物回收的數量為 560 萬噸，低於透過掩埋方式處理的家庭廢棄物為 650 萬噸。

2. 下列哪個句子最適合作為本文的標題？

   (A) 澳洲製造許多垃圾，而我們也是垃圾貢獻者之一。

   (B) 今日圖表：澳洲的垃圾從何而來？

   (C) 餐廳、辦公室、零售與製造業─澳洲的主要汙染源。

   (D) 誰應該為澳洲每日的垃圾負責？

   此圖表分析澳洲廢棄物的來源、資源回收情形與垃圾掩埋的噸數，故選(B)。

3. 下列何者會覺得在工作時此圖表有很大的用處？

   (A) 環境記者。

   (B) 商業分析師。

   (C) 體育特派員。

   (D) 軟體製造商。

   本文圖表羅列澳洲垃圾的來源、資源回收與掩埋情形，屬於環境議題，因此環境記者應會覺得它最有用，故選(A)。

4. 下列關於圖表的敘述何者為非？

   (A) 澳洲家庭並非最大的垃圾來源。

   (B) 商業行為是澳洲最大的垃圾製造者。

   (C) 90% 的建築拆除業垃圾都被再利用與再製造。

   (D) 澳洲的垃圾回收量超過垃圾掩埋量。

   根據圖表顯示，建築與拆除業仍有 710 萬噸是用掩埋方式處理，故選(C)。

5. 從該圖表可以推論出什麼？

   (A) 澳洲同一時間正在執行幾項重大建設。

   (B) 澳洲政府在執行每日垃圾減量上有困難。

   (C) 就資源回收而言，澳洲家庭仍需再加把勁。

   (D) 澳洲人是世界上最大的垃圾製造源。

   就回收量與掩埋量的數值相比較，工商業和建築拆除業的回收量都較高，僅家庭垃圾的回收量比掩埋量還低，可見家庭所生產的垃圾仍以掩埋為主，故選(C)。

Unit 2

1. A　　2. D　　3. D　　4. B
5. Pesticides damage ecosystems, and poisonous heavy metals used to process raw cotton are discharged untreated into local waterways.

本篇說明成衣如何製造，並提到製造過程中工人被剝削的狀況，同時呼籲公平交易 T 恤的重要性。

1. 本海報的目的為何？
  (A) 為呼籲成衣供應鏈中的公平交易概念。
  (B) 為顯示消費者應為童裝付出多少錢。
  (C) 為介紹成衣如何被製造與出售。
  (D) 為解釋為何 T-shirt 可以低價出售。
  　　由表中的 We Need a Fair-Trade T-shirt 可知，此海報的目的在訴求公平交易的成衣，故選(A)。

2. 根據這張海報，下列敘述何者為非？
  (A) 小孩被雇用乃為了降低成衣製造的成本。
  (B) 成衣工人主要為女性及未受教育的人。
  (C) 成衣加工的過程中常造成水汙染。
  (D) 消費者最後得到的衣料完全不含化學物質。
  　　圖中提到 Harmful residues remain in the final fabric，顯示消費者所收到的衣料未必完全不含有害物質，故選(D)。

3. 在看到這張海報後，誰最有可能抗議成衣產業？
  (A) 紡織業。
  (B) 服裝設計師。
  (C) 零售商。
  (D) 棉花農。
  　　本海報主要在為成衣製造過程中被剝削的人發聲，其中提到棉花農的薪水微薄，窮到無法做其他投資，產生惡性循環，因此棉花農應該是這個產業中較弱勢的族群，故選(D)。

4. 從該幅海報中可推論出什麼？
  (A) 越來越多的消費者開始在乎市場上買得到的成衣是如何被製造的。
  (B) 我們所穿的成衣是透過剝削勞工的製造商們做的。
  (C) 人造棉被使用在成衣市場上已經是公開的秘密。
  (D) 衣服可被高價出售乃是因為原物料價格上漲。
  　　由表格中的論述可知，童工和婦女在高工時以及危險的環境下工作，也沒有權利要求更好的薪資，更別說受教育的權利，可見勞工被剝削狀況的嚴重性，故選(B)。

5. 根據本幅海報，成衣產業如何影響環境？
  圖中提到殺蟲劑會毀壞生態系統 (Cotton is grown using pesticides that damage ecosystems)、未處理過的有毒金屬會被排放到水道中 (Raw cotton is processed using poisonous heavy metals that are discharged untreated into local waterways)。

Unit 3

1. C　2. A　3. C　4. B
5. To show how the company makes an effort to minimize its impact on the environment and maximize its sustainable value to fulfill its CSR.

本篇為介紹 SANMIN 公司如何實踐企業的社會責任 (CSR)，並提供了各式數據來呈現他們在永續經營上所做的努力。

1. 下列何者最能描述本篇文章？
   (A) SANMIN 是一家製造高品質金屬製品的頂尖公司。
   (B) SANMIN 努力在沒落的傳統產業求生存。
   (C) SANMIN 在維持永續發展上不遺餘力。
   (D) SANMIN 這幾年來已發展成為營收可觀的企業。
   文章及圖表都著重在 SANMIN 公司對於永續發展 (sustainability development) 的努力，故選(C)。

2. SANMIN 公司如何呈現自己在永續表現上的企業社會責任？
   (A) 藉由提出數據。
   (B) 藉由講述公司歷史。
   (C) 藉由給顧客津貼。
   (D) 藉由獎勵股東。
   圖中顯示了 SANMIN 公司在企業永續經營上的成果數據，例如減少百分之二十的碳排放、降低百分之五的能源密集度等等，故選(A)。

3. 根據 2023 年 SANMIN 公司所顯示的永續表現圖表，下列何者未包含在該公司的永續發展中？
   (A) 員工福祉。
   (B) 與社區合作。
   (C) 發現再生能源。
   (D) 投資公平交易與生物貿易。
   根據圖表，SANMIN 公司花費了 650 萬美金在社區投資以及津貼補助上，並請大約 10,000 名員工加入社區志工的行列；且 SANMIN 公司在生物貿易上推動了兩項新措施；而根據報告，SANMIN 公司的職場重大傷重率 (DART rate) 降低了 26%，損失工作天數率 (lost workday rate) 提升了 26%。最後，圖表中僅提到 82% 購買的電來自再生來源 (82% of purchased electricity from renewable sources)，並非發現再生能源，故選(C)。

4. 下列何者最不可能對本篇文章感興趣？
   (A) 那些從事環境永續性運動的人。
   (B) 專門揭露公司醜聞的記者。
   (C) 非常關注環保的積極份子。
   (D) 重視公司形象的股東們。
   圖表及文章皆呈現 SANMIN 公司的良好形象，包括他們如何實踐社會責任，與經營對環境的永續發展，因此記者無法在這篇文章中找到醜聞，故選(B)。

5. 為何 SANMIN 公司要用一張圖表展現它在 2023 年中所有的永續表現？
   文中提到 SANMIN 正盡全力將對環境的影響降至最低，並最佳化自己的永續價值，以實踐其企業社會責任。

Unit 4

> 1. Lack of vegetation; heat released by traffic; long-wave radiation is reflected from walls back to street level.
> 2. A 3. D 4. C 5. B

圖一列出都市與郊區的溫度變化，圖二則是列出都市形成熱島效應 (UHI) 的因素。

1. 都市熱島效應 (UHI) 是一種當市區溫度比近郊溫度還高時會產生的一種現象。列出發生此現象的三個原因。

   圖二中一共列出了六種都市熱島效應形成的原因：長波輻射從高牆反射到路面、建材儲存太陽熱能並在晚上釋放、缺乏植被以及樹蔭、交通工具所產生的熱能、人為活動所產生的熱能，以及因為高樓將空氣困在街道中，導致城市的風速減弱，以上六種都是會造成都市熱島效應的原因。

2. Joanne 今早參加了一場會議，且講者在他的演講中用到了這兩張圖表。下列何者有可能是他這場演講的標題？
   (A) 人類活動帶來的不自然熱能
   (B) 熱浪所造成的災難
   (C) 近幾年溫室效應所造成的有害影響
   (D) 植被分布有多重要

   由圖一可知，市區的溫度比郊區高，而圖二在解釋市區溫度較高的人為因素，故這兩張圖的主題為(A)。

3. 根據本文，關於都市熱島效應何者為真？
   (A) 它不只發生在城市，也發生在鄉村地區。
   (B) 它主要是跟都市中的高樓有關。
   (C) 它導致郊外氣溫較高。
   (D) 它是一種熱氣困在市區時發生的現象。

   都市熱島效應的成因很多，例如圖表中提到的，建築材料會吸收太陽產生的熱能，並在晚上釋放 (building materials store solar heat and release it at night) 及高樓將熱氣儲存在市區街道上 (tall buildings trap air in the streets)，都說明熱氣被困在城市裡，故選(D)。

4. 圖表一中，為何公園裡的氣溫較城郊的住宅區要低？
   (A) 樹木可以幫助提升風速與蒸發作用。
   (B) 在綠地上沒有長波輻射。
   (C) 植被幫助減少熱能與提供陰涼處。
   (D) 綠色能吸收來自城市的熱能。

   由圖二可知，缺乏植被 (lack of vegetation)、缺乏蒸發冷卻 (lack of evaporate cooling) 和缺乏陰涼處 (shading) 會導致 UHI 的發生。公園裡有植被與樹蔭，溫度當然較低，而住宅區中因建築相對較多，會吸收熱氣，因此城郊的住宅區在圖一的溫度才會比公園高，故選(C)。

5. 下列何者無法幫助減少都市熱島效應的衝擊？
   (A) 搭乘大眾運輸去上課或上班。
   (B) 建造大型建築並漆成綠色。
   (C) 節約能源和減少碳排放量。
   (D) 降低都市發展並種更多樹。

   圖二有提到都市中的熱氣來源有交通 (heat released by traffic)，故搭乘大眾運輸可以幫助降低來自交通的熱氣；而且其中一大熱源就是來自於人類活動，若能降低電能、冷暖氣等的使用，就不會加劇都市熱島效應；最後由於熱氣就是因為被建築物的材料所吸收，而且高樓會將熱氣困在都市內，因此減少高樓以及多種樹都有助於改善都市熱島效應。只有將所有建築物漆成綠色並無實質效用，故選(B)。

Unit 5

> 1. C→A→D→B 2. D 3. C
> 4. We should ask people if they need help before we help them; nature usually has a reason for doing so.

本篇除了定義「變態」一詞外，也詳細說明了毛蟲蛻變成蝴蝶的變態過程。

1. 將 A 至 D 敘述依蝴蝶的生命週期排出正確順序。

蝴蝶成蟲經過交配過程後會在葉子上產卵，之後毛蟲 (幼蟲) 就會從卵中孵出來；接著幼蟲會將自己倒掛，並隨著身體縮小變厚，開始結繭，並在蟲蛹階段開始經歷變態過程，最後破繭而出變成蝴蝶。故正確順序為 C→A→D→B。

2. 根據提供的資訊，下列敘述何者為真？
   (A) 變態僅發生在小昆蟲身上。
   (B) 毛蟲在被孵出來後相當脆弱。
   (C) 蝴蝶是在蛹的階段開始繁殖下一代。
   (D) 繭是一種用來覆蓋昆蟲的外殼。

   根據本圖對變態的定義，有提到此過程會發生在昆蟲或其他動物身上 (Metamorphosis is a huge transformation or change in the form of an insect or other kinds of animals.)，由此可知並非僅發生在小昆蟲身上；現有資訊中並未提到毛蟲孵化之後會變得脆弱；從這張圖可知，蝴蝶必須變成成蟲後交配方可繁殖下一代，而非在蛹的階段繁殖。根據 its body shortening and thickening until it forms a hard case called cocoon around itself 這句話可知，繭是一種覆蓋在昆蟲外面的殼，故選(D)。

3. 本篇文章中蝴蝶發生了什麼事？
   (A) 牠因為牠的翅膀被男人剪掉而變殘廢。
   (B) 牠在破繭而出後就變得非常有活力。
   (C) 牠沒有經歷過必要的掙扎來破繭而出。
   (D) 牠沒有歷經變態過程來變成蝴蝶成蟲。

由文章中描述可知，這隻蝴蝶並未靠自己的力量破繭而出，而是直接從男人為牠剪的洞口中出來，故選(C)。

4. 本篇文章背後隱含什麼訊息？

本題學生可以從各種面向討論。參考答案如下：我們在幫助他人之前應該要先詢問對方是否有需要；大自然會這麼做，通常都有它的道理在。

Unit 6

1. C　　2. C　　3. D　　4. B
5. Kenny did not trust in his team and it is definitely less likely for his team members to be loyal to him.

本文是一篇職場問題諮商，內容講述上司被離職員工在背後中傷，也因此開始對下屬產生不信任感。

1. 我們可以得知什麼關於本篇文章的訊息？
   (A) 這是一則熱門網路新聞的留言。
   (B) 這是一個 Kenny 公司的行銷專案。
   (C) 這是一篇與職場人際關係有關的心理論壇文章。
   (D) 這是一篇對 Eliz Leyn 新出版品的書評。
   最上方標題為「面對工作團隊中的垃圾話」(Confronting Trash Talk in Your Work Team)，並從提出的問題可以得知，發問者和職場上的同事們處於緊張且不信任的關係，故選(C)。

2. 為何 Kenny 向 Eliz Leyn 尋求建議？
   (A) Kenny 無法忍受任何來自同事的垃圾話。
   (B) Kenny 很生氣他的同事們升官了。
   (C) Kenny 不知道如何處理前同事的行為。
   (D) Kenny 試著找出一些挑釁的方法來回應同事。
   由 Kenny 提出的問題可知，他的一位離職同事向其他組員說他壞話，使他變得不再信任這些人，但也不知道該怎麼處理這個狀況，故選(C)。

3. 閱讀本篇文章後，下列何者是 Leyn 給 Kenny 的建議？
   (A) 她建議 Kenny 解散小組並澄清誤會。
   (B) 她建議 Kenny 跟每一個團隊成員對話。
   (C) 她建議 Kenny 站在離職員工的立場。
   (D) 她引導 Kenny 保持客觀且專注在事件本身而非人上面。

Leyn 建議 Kenny 好好想一想每一位團隊成員正向的特質與行為，並建議他將自己的成見與這件事分開，要針對事情處理而非針對人，故選(D)。

4. 畫底線的「perpetrator」一字是指什麼？
   (A) Kenny 所面臨的負面回饋。
   (B) 對 Kenny 做出糟糕行為的人。
   (C) 使用指控話語的人。
   (D) Kenny 被他同事罵的真相。
   由「倘若這件事一直持續，你將需要正面迎戰＿＿＿來結束它！小心準備與那個人的對話 (If the uncomfortable situation continues, you'll need to confront the perpetrator to end it! Prepare carefully for the conversation with that person」可知，這裡的空格應該要填一個和 Kenny 敵對的對象，故選(B)。

5. 為何 Eliz Leyn 提到「信任與忠誠是互諒互讓的關係」？她對 Kenny 暗示了什麼？
   英文中的 two-way street 為互相幫助的關係，而非單方面做出努力即可達成。她暗示 Kenny 若只會一味懷疑下屬，當然不可能獲得下屬的忠誠。

Unit 7

1. Riding a bike; travelling on foot/walking.
2. C   3. A   4. D

本篇為一期刊內容。圖表一說明不同車種與乘客每公里的碳排放量。圖表二則描述 2014 年到 2018 年間燃油與溫室氣體排放量之間的關係。

1. 根據圖表一，哪兩種運輸模式對環境最友善？

圖表一中的 bicycle 與 pedestrian 在碳排放量上的數據都是每公里 8 公克，遠低於其他運輸模式，故此題答案為 Riding a bike 和 travelling on foot/walking。

2. 根據以上兩篇節錄，這篇期刊最不可能是在討論哪一個議題？

(A) 溫室氣體排放量自 2014 年起降低的原因。

(B) 不同的運輸方式對二氧化碳總排放量的影響。

(C) **溫室氣體排放如何使氣候變遷更惡化。**

(D) 燃油在降低溫室氣體量上的角色。

這兩個段落都在討論碳排放量與交通工具的關係，並無提及氣候變遷是否惡化與為何惡化，故選(C)。

3. 下列何者與畫底線的「negligible」一字在字義上最為接近？

(A) **很小而且不值得擔憂。**

(B) 太重要以至於不能被忽略。

(C) 較其他顯而易見。

(D) 有害且對人類危險。

根據圖表，最高和最低的碳排放量分別為自小客車與單車。再由描述「然而 (while) 開自小客車，每位乘客在每公里所製造出的二氧化碳排放量最為顯著」可知，騎腳踏車排放出「微不足道」的二氧化碳，故選(A)。

4. 下列何者最能敘述這兩篇節錄文章的資訊？

(A) 解決都市交通問題的最好辦法為要求所有行人騎腳踏車。

(B) 共乘數量的增加可以解釋二氧化碳排放量自 2014 年開始下降的原因。

(C) 改變一個城市的大眾運輸工具方式會導致較高的油價。

(D) **電動車在幫助降低溫室氣體排放上扮演關鍵的角色。**

根據圖表二，自 2014 年起燃油使用量降低，而溫室氣體排放量也降低，再加上圖表二上方文字敘述，Nearly 96% of the bus companies are now funded to buy electric vehicles。可以得知電動車逐漸取代部分交通運輸，燃油需求不再那麼高，碳排放量也會跟著降低，故選(D)。

Unit 8

1. C　2. D　3. A　4. B　5. 略。

本篇介紹何謂炸彈氣旋 (bomb cyclone)。除了介紹炸彈氣旋如何產生外，也提到炸彈氣旋讓北美洲的氣候變得異常。

1. 本文主要關於什麼？
   (A) 一種新發現的武器。
   (B) 一份政治報告。
   (C) 一種天氣現象。
   (D) 一個災害預測。

   > 全文都在討論炸彈氣旋 (bomb cyclone) 的成因與發生時所伴隨的天氣特徵，故選(C)。

2. 下列何者並非形成炸彈氣旋的條件之一？
   (A) 一定是低氣壓系統。
   (B) 暴風雨迅速增強。
   (C) 氣壓在 24 小時內下降 24 百帕 (以上)。
   (D) 必定伴隨著颶風。

   > 炸彈氣旋會伴隨著強風或暴雪，沿海積水與颶風般威力的狂風。這是炸彈氣旋所導致的天氣狀況，而非炸彈氣旋形成的條件，故選(D)。

3. 當炸彈氣旋發生時，下列何者不會發生？
   (A) 氣溫 (上升)。
   (B) 暴風雪 (增加)。
   (C) 降雪。
   (D) 淹水。

   > 炸彈氣旋發生時，北美的氣溫反而下降而非上升，故選(A)。

4. 何者最有可能於下一段中討論？
   (A) 如何精準預測炸彈氣旋。
   (B) 造成這幾年氣候變得如此極端的原因。
   (C) 下一個炸彈氣旋橫掃美國的時間。
   (D) 美國東部的總降雪量是否會破紀錄。

   > 文末有提到全球氣溫上升，但異常的氣候變化卻使美國及加拿大特別寒冷，依照這個邏輯，下一段比較有可能探究極端氣候 (形成) 原因，故選(B)。

5. 在讀完本文之後，你同意有些人評論「炸彈氣旋」是一種形容天氣現象的誇張說法嗎？為何 (不)？

   此題為開放性問題，可以由不同面向討論。通常氣象的術語應該要精準，而此類的氣旋也有其嚴格的對應標準。用「炸彈」二字或許會有誤導之嫌，但炸彈氣旋發生後所造成的天然災害也的確如同被炸彈轟炸過一般，用「炸彈」二字的確可以迅速讓一般民眾了解這個氣旋的威力，提早做好防災準備。

Unit 9

1. A　2. C　3. Seattle.　4. D

本篇為美國 2017 年前七大遊民人口數城市分布圖以及人數 (圖表一)。

1. 哪一資訊無法在圖表一中找到？
   (A) **2017 年美國無家可歸的人口總數。**
   (B) 美國遊民人口的城市排名。
   (C) 美國遊民人口的分布狀況。
   (D) 製作這張圖表的政府部門。

   本表列出美國遊民人口數量的前七大城市分佈，圖表中可以看到七個城市的排名、分布狀況以及資料來源，但並無提供全美遊民人口的總數，故選(A)。

2. 下列敘述何者正確？
   (A) 紐約市多年來一直有最多的遊民人口。
   (B) 聖荷西的遊民人口只被哥倫比亞地區超過。
   (C) **洛杉磯 2017 年有第二大遊民人口數。**
   (D) 舊金山在 2017 年擁有美國最少的遊民人口。

   圖表一僅列出 2017 年的狀況，故無法得知紐約市這幾年來的情形如何；而聖荷西在此張圖中排名第六名，只有超過舊金山，剩餘五個地區的遊民人口數都超越聖荷西；最後舊金山在此圖中是最後一名，表示是全美的第七名，而非全美最少。此圖表是全美前七大遊民人口數排名，因此若在這張圖表中排名第二名，表示在全美排名亦為第二名，故選(C)。

3. 以上描述引用自美國一份當地報紙。根據圖表一與這段文字，空格中應該填入哪一個城市？

   本格後面有 ranking third in the number of not only the homeless but also the unsheltered homeless，表示該城市在圖表中為第三名，故答案為西雅圖 (Seattle)。

4. 下列哪一個統計圖最能解釋上面所描述的現象？

   文中提到從 2007 年起，遊民人數一直在攀升，到 2017 年已增加 47%，故(B)、(C)錯；到了 2017 年，unsheltered 的人數已經達到 5,485 人，故(A)錯。(D)符合此兩項，且相較 2016 年與 2017 年的數據，也符合 21% 的成長，故選(D)。

Unit 10

1. E　2. D　3. A　4. B

本篇說明位於華盛頓州的 Rattlesnake Hills 坍方的情形，圖表一是 Rattlesnake Hills 的地理位置，圖表二則是坍方地區的岩層分布狀況與坍方方向。

1. 閱讀圖表一。我們可以在哪一地點 (地點 A 至地點 F) 找到文中畫底線的採石場 (quarry)？

   文中提到 a landslide has been observed occurring above the north of a quarry, bounded by Thorp Rd. to the south and west，表示這個採石場的北邊發生了坍方，且它的南邊跟西邊與 Thorp Rd. 為界。加上 Thorp Rd. 跟 I-82 公路很相近，公路若也遭逢坍方，就會影響採石場南方的房屋，所以可推論採石場所在的位置為 E。

2. 根據上方描述，一旦發生坍方，圖表一裡面哪一個地點最不可能受到影響？

   由圖表二可知，坍方是由北向南滑行，因此所有選項中最不可能被波及的地區為北方的 F，故選(D)。

3. 下列哪一標題最有可能在這篇文章中的下個段落被討論？

   (A) 為了坍方所採取的預防措施。

   (B) 造成河川下游淹水的原因。

   (C) Rattlesnake Hills 周遭的生態系統。

   (D) 採石場與 Yakima River 的關係。

   本段最後都在說坍方最有可能的走向與影響範圍有多廣。在邏輯上的安排，接著討論該怎麼預防會比較合理，故選(A)。

4. 哪一個字在字義上最接近圖表二中的「failure」？

   (A) 圍堵。

   (B) 崩塌。

   (C) 採石場。

   (D) 情節。

圖二在描述土石滑移的方向與岩層結構。由圖二可知，failure surface 為崩裂土石與主體結構的交界處，因此 failure 在此為「崩塌」之意，故選(B)。